PUFFIN BO

# johnny hart's heroes

David Metzenthen was born in Melbourne in 1958. Since abandoning employment as an advertising copywriter he has devoted himself to writing fiction for adults and younger readers. David has lived in New Zealand and travelled within Australia and overseas to gather information and ideas for this work.

The idea for *Johnny Hart's Heroes* grew from the love of a landscape where old woolsheds stand near older gum trees, kelpies chase stubborn sheep, and work is often as hard to get as it is to do properly. A concern for young Australians striving to achieve independence and satisfaction was a major force behind the writing of this novel.

David lives in Melbourne with his wife and two small children, Ella and Liam.

*Johnny Hart's Heroes* was the winner of the Ethel Turner Prize in the 1996 New South Wales Premier's Literary Awards.

Other books by David Metzenthen

*Danger Wave*
*Lee Spain*
*Brocky's Bananagram*
*Roadie*
*Animal Instinct*
*Finn and the Big Guy*

# johnny
## hart's
# heroes

david metzenthen

PUFFIN BOOKS

*The author wishes to thank Frank Noble*
*for the use of his immaculate 1943 Dodge Utility*
*which appears on the front cover of this book.*

Puffin Books
Penguin Books Australia Ltd
487 Maroondah Highway, PO Box 257
Ringwood, Victoria 3134, Australia
Penguin Books Ltd
Harmondsworth, Middlesex, England
Viking Penguin, A Division of Penguin Books USA Inc.
375 Hudson Street, New York, New York 10014, USA
Penguin Books Canada Limited
10 Alcorn Avenue, Toronto, Ontario, Canada M4V 3B2
Penguin Books (N.Z.) Ltd
Cnr Rosedale and Airborne Roads, Albany, Auckland, New Zealand

First published by Penguin Books Australia, 1996
10 9 8 7 6 5 4 3
Copyright © David Metzenthen, 1996

Typeset in 11/14½ Weiss by Post Typesetters, Brisbane
Made and printed in Australia by Australian Print Group, Maryborough, Victoria

National Library of Australia
Cataloguing-in-Publication data:

Metzenthen, David.
   Johnny Hart's heroes.

   ISBN 0 14 037939 8.

   I. Title.

A823.3

For Russ and Nance Dalkin, 'Westgate', Ararat.

Thanks always for letting me run wild
in your paddocks.

# one

I swear your knuckles really do go white. I'm watching my best buddy, Ralph Edward Kiddle, fighting a mad bulldozer driver and I'm gripping a roll of tickets so tightly my knuckles have gone bone bloodless white.

Ralphy boxes on his toes, attacking then skilfully defending – but the fat-armed bulldozer driver fights only in forward gear, never giving ground as he grunts and swears and swings. Again and again Ralph hits him, smacking sprays of sweat off his face and ribs, but the bulldozer driver won't go down. I glance at our boss, Danny Barley, who looks like a cheapskate undertaker in a black satin shirt, complete with a Texan drawstring tie flashing a bit of fake opal at his throat.

'Bad fight,' I yell over the rolling roar of the crowd. 'Gussy shoulda fought this guy, not Ralph. That other bloke's heaps bigger.'

Danny shrugs. He gave up feeling anything for anyone years ago.

'Stick to sellin' tickets, Lal. Leave the fightin' to the boys.'

Sure, okay, maybe I don't know much about boxing – but I

do know welterweights don't fight fat middleweights. Or they shouldn't; but out here Bush Rules rule. You fight the fella who's standing in front of you.

The bulldozer driver charges, overrunning Ralphy's delicate advantage of speed and skill with brute force. It's the turning point of the fight. Ralph gets hit hard, his head slapped to the left. His hands drop and the next wild right catches him flush in the middle of the face. Down on one knee he goes, a gloved hand resting on the slack middle rope. Dazed and wobbly, Ralphy tries to stand, blood spilling from his nose and washing down over his mouth and chin.

I will him to stay down and take the ten count, but he doesn't. A deep ache fills me; as if the punches have not only battered my best friend's face, but hurt his very soul. And mine as well.

Ralph pushes himself to his feet, hoists his gloves, then gets hit again, this time collapsing sideways to lie flat out on dirty canvas. It's over. Under the white lights his skin is shiny brown and his nose leaks blood like dark oil. Sideshow tent fighting. If there's a harder way to make a living I don't know about it.

Danny Barley springs up into the ring, shiny black boot heels reflecting half moons of electric light. He congratulates the bulldozer driver and hands him a fan of red notes, the prize for knocking our fighter out. Ralph makes it to his feet and stands crookedly in the dazed, lonely world of the beaten boxer.

Danny, now with a lit cigarette, shouts out into hot, noisy, restless air, 'On behalf of Barley's Travellin' Outback Boxing Show – ' He waits for the noise level to drop one per cent. 'Thanks for comin' along tonight, fellas.' He wags his head, a showman's show of 'no hard feelings'. 'Of course tomorrow evening there'll be other tough punchers here to take ya on, and real money if ya can go the distance or win the fight. Take it easy and g'night.'

Good night? I don't think so.

Ralph and I sit beside a leaky tap in the dark, him with a broken nose and me with a broken – heart? Nope, not yet, anyway. The damn fly on my jeans has had it. Today, I've got to say, just ain't our day.

I push up next to Ralph, my pale bare girl's arm softly muscling in on his hard smooth brown one. For a moment we both look down at the same patch of dusty red dirt. Light from the carnival makes it look sickly orange.

'Ralph,' I say quietly, 'it's time to quit.' I touch his arm. 'Either you tell Danny or I will.'

Ralph lifts his head, not looking at me but at the back of Danny Barley's Travelling Outback Boxing Show, a big green tent where I've watched him win and lose fights five nights a week since last November. Four months of travelling around tough Queensland bush towns. Seems like four years. Hard to believe I ever did have a boring little pub job in Goondiwindi, even harder to believe last year I was lying on the beach at home at Delaney Bay, with long salt-bleached blonde hair and the sea nibbling at my toes. Not now. This is where looking for adventure gets you – into a tight, grubby, miserable corner.

Curly black hair slips down Ralph's forehead and there's a wad of bloody white cotton against his nose. He slumps back, all energy and fight pummelled out of him. I try again.

'I think you're finished with the fighting, Ralph. It's just too bloody hard.'

'But I like it,' he says tiredly, then launches into the boxer's prayer. 'I can win a title, I know it.' He spits another wobbly blob of crimson blood into the gully trap, then turns on the spluttering tap. 'Maybe get on TV.' He nods. 'Fight Night on Sky Channel. It'd be big dough, that's what Danny reckons. Says he knows blokes down south who can fix it.'

Then Danny Barley's a liar. And a user. Titles aren't won in sideshows. Sky television wouldn't touch a tent boxer like Ralph Kiddle with a barge pole, whatever a barge pole is ... Jesus, who's Danny trying to kid? Ralph, I guess. I try not to watch the revolting bloody blobs slide down the black drain. Ralphy says he likes fighting. Likes it. I laugh an unhappy laugh and lay a hand on the fine curve of the back of his neck.

He's slimly built is Ralph, shaped like a diamond from the hips up, and on the tall side of medium. He's fit too, with the long fine muscles of a greyhound, even if the big red gloves he fights in look too bulky for his arms. He's not a slugger or a brawler, Ralph Kiddle, he's a boxer – even if I wish he was anything else but.

'You're an idiot, Ralphy,' I say, and pull him close, our heads clonking like a couple of ripe coconuts. 'But a nice one. Too nice to keep up with this garbage, eh?' I touch the sodden swab. 'Give it away, hey?'

Ralph folds his arms, fists on elbows, elbows on knees, smears of dried blood on his wrists like finger paint.

'I used to beat everyone.'

I love Ralph's voice. Every word he softens a little, like someone drawing might soften a line by using charcoal.

'I always had more go than the others,' he tells me. 'Back home I never got done once. Even down in Melbourne. Well, maybe once.'

I feel the muscles in Ralphy's side loosen as he sags. I rub my hand up and down his bare back, feeling knobbly bone under warm skin. My friend, my friend.

'Out here's different, mate,' I say. 'You know it is. This ain't real boxing, this is just brawling.' What do I say next? How do you tell someone else to get a new job? How do you tell someone they can't afford to keep on losing? 'You'll sort something out,' I add, 'but this has gotta stop.' I touch his swollen face.

He looks at me, battered, exhausted, injured.

'Yeah, sure, maybe – ' He holds up a fist with the grimy bloody bandages all fighters wear under their gloves. 'But what else am I gonna do? I can't do anythin' else, Lal.' He lets the hand fall to slap loosely on blood-smeared red boxing shorts.

I look at a rainbow scatter of tossed beer cans for inspiration, but get none.

'Why don't you just go home for a while?' I suggest. 'To Echuca? To the Murray? Get a job in the sawmill again? Hey, couldn't you maybe work on the council with your old man?'

'Nah.' Ralph stares down at some place or something I can't see. 'Can't go back. Can't do it.'

I have another try, leaning towards him, my hands on his bare bony knees.

'Course you can. Why not? You love the river, Ralph, and the bush. That's your people's place down there. Your dad's there, your brother, sisters, cousins. Must be something you can do to get away from this. Geez, just go on the dole.'

Ralph's shoulders go up then down.

'Nah, can't. I wouldn't mind but – ' He glances at me, our eyes locking like cogs. He grins uncertainly. 'Maybe there might be a bit of trouble waitin' down there for me, Lal.'

'Trouble?' I ask, probably looking as puzzled as I sound. 'What sort of trouble? Hold up the stagecoach, did you?' I expect to see his eyes flick up to mine, then he'll present me with a grin that'll show white teeth with one black gap.

He does neither. He smiles oddly down at the dirt, then out into the darkness.

'Nah, just some trouble. Guess I'll stay here for a while.' Now he shows me his face, worry lingering despite his efforts, a tightening of his mouth and eyelids. 'Be all right, eh? I'll get home some other time.'

I'm not sure what to say. Nothing's as straightforward as it seemed two minutes ago. This talk of trouble makes it seem like I have to leap back across a big ditch to get back to territory I feel safe on. I leap.

'No, it won't be bloody all right. You'll get clobbered here one night and wake up a vegie. Give it up, Ralph, please.' I mean it. Too many hard hits and a boxer's brain'll rattle for the rest of his natural life. 'What sort of trouble was it anyway?'

Ralphy looks at me, looks at the canvas walls of Danny Barley's tent.

'Ah, just some trouble. I didn't start it.' He fiddles with the eyelets of his boxing boot, light picking out his cheekbone, shoulder, elbow, fingers poking out of filthy bandages. 'Wasn't my fault, either.' He looks up. 'Not somethin' you really need to know about.'

'Okay,' I say, barging on, 'if you didn't start it and it wasn't your fault, then forget it. Surely you can go home?' I watch him.

Ralph draws his knees up, surrounds them with his arms, sharp elbows sticking out. 'I can't, Lal, so don't ask me no more, okay?'

'Okay, I won't.'

Anyway, what's so special about not being able to go home? Hell, I don't want to go home, either. Of course I *could*, but certain things have got to change before I ever would. Me, for instance. Again I go back to safe ground.

'You've got to quit fighting, Ralph. It's a bloody deathtrap.'

Ralph laughs, the usual cheeky, singing tones surfacing in his voice again.

'Hey, I got my friends here, Lal. Anythin's better than bein' on your own, eh?' He smiles a swollen smile. 'I'll be okay.' He whips away the cotton swab, as if to show me his nose has miraculously healed. 'See? Good as gold.'

It's not. There's thick black blood on the cotton square and his nose is caked with it. If Ralph stays here I doubt he'll get out alive, or in one piece. He'll fight anyone Danny tells him to. Ralph thinks nothing can touch him, that life goes on forever – but after what I went through with a best friend of mine a while ago, I've got a different story. When Indi Emma Jane got sick, I realised – suddenly words are right there in the air in front of me.

'We'll both quit then, Ralph,' I say. 'I've had enough of watching you go through this stuff. I just realised.' I wave my hand in the direction of the tent. 'Let's go. What d'you say?'

Ralph's arms release his knees. 'Both of us?' He laughs. 'You an' me? And do what?' Good question.

'Who knows?' I say, back to my brilliant best. 'Who cares? We'll getta life. A new one. A better one. Why not?' I'm firing up now. 'There's no law says we can't have some good luck for once, is there?'

Look, maybe I couldn't do anything much to help Indi Emma Jane in the end, but if quitting a dead-end job'll help Ralphy, then hell, I'll quit! A feeling of freedom rises in my head like gas. Underdogs of the world unite! I stand up, holding onto my decision – and the front of my jeans.

'We're gonna go, Kiddle.' I feel like I've fired myself from a cannon with nowhere to land. 'What the hell. Bugger it. We'll find something.' We'd better. I've got about two hundred and fifty bucks to my name.

God. This whole thing is my old man's fault, and my dumb brother's. If they hadn't taught me to drive like a farmer I would never have got the job of towing Danny Barley's caravans from one end of Queensland to the other. Or selling the stupid boxing tent tickets, or cooking everybody's revolting meals. Or being unemployed, again.

But if I hadn't joined the tent I wouldn't have met Ralphy, and I haven't had a friend like him for a long time. That being the case, I figure I've got more to gain and less to lose by quitting than staying. Besides, the dude can make me laugh.

From minute one of day one with Barley's Travelling Outback Boxing Show, Ralph and I got on. There I was in Dinnamulla, big sticks bush Queensland, hot off the Goondiwindi bus, anchored to the dusty car park by my one black bag – and there was Ralphy in the raging midday sun, sent to meet me, skipping-rope over one shoulder, a red can in either hand, saying, 'Hey, if you're Lal, I've gotta Coke for ya.'

I took the Coke and I loved it, and I don't even like Coke all that much. It was that hot.

You know how it is when you meet someone, and the first thing you do is laugh? Ralph and I did; we just clicked, like a couple of happy heeler dogs let loose in the park, one red, one blue. Well, one black, one white, anyway.

Ralphy and I are living proof that opposites attract. I'm white Australian, he's black. I'm from the coast, he's from the bush. I like chips, he likes fish. I'm a loudmouth, Ralph keeps his shut. I cry, he laughs. I'm tight with money, Ralph throws it around. My family's small, Ralph's is big. My temper's fast and fiery, his is slow and dangerous. I keep a rubbishy diary, Ralph likes to read rubbishy westerns – featuring Larry and Stretch.

So we're friends. Nothing more, at least not now – but certainly nothing less. And from here on it's us against the rest; which gives me the feeling that although the boxing's finished, I don't think the fighting's over by a long shot.

I have quit. For the both of us. Ralph has hung up his gloves and I've given Danny back his car keys and *Woman's Weekly Cookbook*, which I never opened anyway. And now I'm stuffing my one black bag with all my clothes and a few doubts.

I look around my little caravan. Its windows are like portholes, my bed like a lumpy life raft. The mirror shows me my freckly face – amazing how pale and big-eyed you look with no hair. Well, I've got hair, but not nearly as much as I used to have. I felt like a change, now I feel bald. What's left is just a crop of pale stubble that shows my head to be shaped exactly like a light bulb. I look like a pixie, if they're also short, flat-chested and skinny.

Outside, caravans are circled as if expecting a raid, and beyond the fence dry paddocks stretch out as never-ending as the sea. This town might have a video store and a laundromat, but it seems a million miles away from civilisation when you've got nowhere planned to go and nothing planned to do.

I pick up my bag and toe open the flimsy door. Goodbye little van, I've dreamed some good dreams between your tinny walls; like, one day I won't have to live in a caravan!

Well, unemployed again. From tuna canning factory to pub to boxing tent in under eighteen months. Wouldn't they be impressed with me back at Delaney Bay High School? Nope, I don't think they would. At school I was like a skipping stone, only touching down every so often and oh-so-lightly – the entire staffroom watching me skim past, probably thinking that like every other stone flying over deep water I'd soon sink without a trace.

And I guess when they heard I was working in the canning

factory at Bermagui I would've been considered a truly lost soul. Well, I'm not – quite. Or yet, even if I'm once again treading water. I lug my bag across open ground, watched by Franky the Shetland pony. The only thing left to do now is give our goodbyes to Looby.

To think, let alone say, Looby Jackson is fat, would be dangerous. Looby is large and heavy, but he is not fat. Looby also has lost most of his front teeth, but one thing he's never lost, thank God, is his temper. Looby Jackson was the resident heavyweight fighter of Danny Barley's boxing show, but he's retired now and looks after Danny's fighters, vehicles and caravans. He's also everybody's favourite uncle.

Loob touches Ralph's swollen nose with super-sized fingers. Looby knows about boxers' broken faces and bodies.

'Not so bad, brother,' he pronounces, his voice like the deep gentle twang of a big didgeridoo. 'He'll mend, if you don't get him busted up again.' Looby puts his hands on the table, making a lump about the size of a small tree stump. 'But I hear you're goin' anyway. What are you fellas gonna do?'

Ralph looks straight at me. Oh, thanks very much. I look at Looby.

'Not sure yet, Loob. Just get out of here first. Things haven't been going real good lately. You know what I mean.'

Beside me Ralph studies his hands, dark against the woodgrain laminex tabletop. He wishes he wasn't here.

Looby Jackson doesn't need me to explain anything about the battering a fighter might take. His cousin, a Queensland lightweight with great prospects, died after a terrible fight in Brisbane. No prospects now for Lightning Lenny Brooks; only a few yellowing newspaper cuttings filling a page-and-a-half of Looby Jackson's big scrapbook.

10

'You're a lovely boxer, Ralph,' the heavyweight adds carefully, 'but tent fightin's no bloody good. Be banned everywhere soon, probably. Even Queensland.' He smiles, his big loose lips sliding back to show baby-pink gums. 'Maybe some people don't think it shows a modern Australia.' Loob taps his temple, a small smooth pan of black skin. 'Most fighters get hurt, brother. And you would've too, sometime. Find somethin' better, eh?'

'That's what I said, Loob,' I say. 'Bit hard, though. Jobs, you know, hard to get.'

Ralph won't look at Looby. When Looby lets a fighter know he's finished it's not a suggestion, it's law. Even Danny 'Dollar' Barley listens when the big guy talks.

'Something else'll crop up,' I toss in, then snap my fingers. 'Today I'm feelin' lucky.' I am?

Looby sighs like a steady westerly wind. He smiles and raises one of his heavy hands.

'Go see Johnny Hart.' He points out of the door of his old caravan. 'I hear he's got somethin' goin'. He's shearin' sheep over the road in that big old tin shed. You can't miss him. He's got one of them steel calipers on his leg.'

And that's how we got to meet John J Hart, the shearer with one bung leg and eyes the colour of broken blue ice. Thanks, Looby. You always did know how to look after your friends, your fighters, and your ex-fighters.

# two

We don't have to travel far to find Johnny Hart. One hundred metres away in the Nellie Nutley Memorial Pavilion he's shearing sheep on a wooden stage, peeling a creamy fleece off an unhappy looking merino. The small crowd is quiet, the loud buzzing of the shears reminds me of Vinny Calypso's barber shop for blokes back home in good old Delaney Bay.

'He's doin' all right for a bloke with a crook leg,' Ralph whispers. 'He's faster than the other fella.'

True. I get the feeling Johnny Hart is an expert at his business. His hand, gripping the silver shearing piece, glides downwards in long sweeps pushed by a right arm lumpy with muscle. Then he straightens up, hairy chested, and tunnel-balls a now very shorn and white sheep out through a small wooden gate.

'I wouldn't mind havin' a go at that,' says Ralph. 'My cousin's a hairdresser. Might run in the family.'

I laugh. If I was a sheep I wouldn't let Ralph near my wool with a hairbrush, let alone a pair of those shears. Ralph reckons that because he can box, bat, kick and run he can also handle any work tool like an expert. I'm not convinced.

'Well, at least a sheep can't ask for its money back,' I say.

Speaking of sheep, this joint is the merino hall of fame. On every wall are pictures and paintings of snooty, curly-horned rams and big tubby ewes, all showing off blue ribbons and home-grown coats you could lose your hands in. The place is dedicated to them; the smell particularly – but it's actually not all that unpleasant. It's a rich, thick, sweet smell. Not dirty, just a good, honest animal pong.

I watch the shearers drag a sheep each from the catching pen. A bell rings and immediately the pace hots up. Johnny Hart's hand pushes out wave after wave of wool, the sheep pressed against a knee or held still until it's also rudely shoved away to join its ice-cream-white buddies.

The other shearer finishes, and he and John Hart shake hands, smiling sweatily at each other like a couple of tennis players across the net. Around Ralph and I the crowd clap politely then stand, their seats snapping up helpfully to put themselves away, and in a minute or so the Nellie Nutley Pavilion is close to being empty. A short show is a good show I guess. I stand. I wish I was taller; people take you more seriously.

'I'll do the talking,' I say to Ralph. 'If we need a couple of little white lies, I'm the one to tell 'em, okay?'

Ralph's eyes half close, his lips flatten. 'Yeah, and get sprung. And then we'll really be buggered.'

'Okay, no lies.' Whoops! I think that might just turn out to be one.

We make our way up to the stage; the place reminding me of a school assembly hall, our riding boots banging across wooden boards, a bad-tempered portrait of the Queen frowning down on us. On the stage the two shearers are talking, towels draped around their shoulders although the Nellie Nutley Pavilion is hot and humid.

'You right there?' says this Johnny Hart to me, his canvas waterbag down by his side as if it's a briefcase.

Stopping a short distance from the shearers I introduce myself and Ralph, and mention Looby Jackson's name. I then bluntly ask Mr Johnny Hart if there might be, er, a couple of jobs available around the place. He crosses beefy arms. If he had a piece of grass handy he'd chew it. The Nellie Nutley Pavilion fills with silence. Johnny Hart sizes us up – for coffins, maybe.

'You're lookin' for work?' he says, as if we're looking for trouble.

Haven't I already said that?

'Yeah, we've just finished up with Barley's boxing tent,' I explain. 'Ralph's given up fighting and I've flicked my job as driver and, er, cook. Looby just mentioned you might have something going.'

In the distance I can hear the clunk-dink of the shooting gallery. Standing here, I must admit I feel a bit like a tin duck myself, waiting to be knocked over. Asking for a job puts you in a very exposed position – when you haven't got much to offer except a pair of hands, the clothes you stand up in, and the desire not to starve to death. We wait. Johnny Hart obviously doesn't do much thinking out loud. The other shearer, a small red-headed fella, packs away a polished shearing handpiece then changes shoes, about to skedaddle.

'Good luck with the trip,' he says to Johnny. 'Hope it works out for yers. Someone's gotta have a go.'

Johnny Hart nods. 'Yeah, thanks, Cliff. Buy you a beer when I get back.'

The shearer leaves, nodding tautly to Ralph and me. I wait, wondering exactly what sort of job this Johnny might have going. And if he's the sort of person I want to work for. He puts out a hard vibe, the sort of guy who'd never borrow anything from anybody, or lend stuff out, either. Self-reliant. Down the line. All the way.

'So you're a tent fighter, Ralph?' Johnny stands hands on hips, an old watch with a sweaty blue band tight around his left wrist. The caliper makes him look tougher and stronger, like a car with a rusty old bullbar. 'Hard way to make a quid.'

Ralph shrugs. 'Too hard, maybe. Sometimes ya get a hiding.'

'Only,' I put in, 'because half the blokes he's had to fight have outweighed him by twenty bloody kilos.' I decide it's time to lay cards on the table. 'So here we are, Mr Hart, lookin' for work. And we'll take on just about anything.'

The shearer nods, then limps away, calipered leg swinging out, to where his handpiece is resting, hanging down from a long silver rod jointed like an elbow. He disconnects the handpiece and wraps it in half a flannel shirt. Above his head metal flywheels glint, the thick inner spokes painted bright red.

'What'd Looby tell yers?' He talks down at the floor as he packs up, sweat soaking his singlet front and back.

'Not much,' I say cautiously. 'He only mentioned you might have something going. Didn't say what.'

Johnny Hart walks back to us, putting his flannel parcel into a beaten-up leather bag that used to be square and used to be brown.

'What d'you know about droving? As in sheep.'

Droving?

'Driving I know about,' I say, 'but droving, not a lot.'

Understatement. I press on. 'Drovers have to eat, though, don't they? I can cook and Ralph can ride a horse, can't you, mate?' This last offering could turn out to be one of those little lies I was talking about earlier.

'Yeah,' says Ralph, 'I can ride a bit. And Lal's a gun driver. She's never had a prang.'

Not entirely true. I did back into a camel in Longreach once – although no one knows about that, apart from the camel, I guess.

Johnny holds his old leather bag as if it's a portable lie detector.

'So, you're not in trouble with the law or anything, are you? I can't have people like that.'

'Hell no,' I say quickly. 'I mean, we've been workin'. We haven't had the time to get into strife.' I laugh, to show that last bit was a joke.

'No trouble,' says Ralph not very convincingly.

Johnny Hart puts his lie detector down, bending low enough for me to see that not only is his hair wavy on top, it's also thinning out a bit. He straightens up, grandpa-slow.

'I need people who can stick out a long, hot, dirty trip. I don't even know how long.' He hooks big hands into the waistband of green work pants, his wrists three times as thick as mine. 'I can't have you if you'll take off in three days because you want a shower.' He looks at Ralph and me as if he's suggesting we walk away.

'We're tough enough,' I say, hoping I sound it. 'And we've got references from the tent, and I've got another lot from the Station Hotel in Goondiwindi.'

Ralph says nothing. Anybody can see he's hard as ti-tree. His eyes are fighter's eyes; eyes that measure strength and ability, as alert as radar. And his arms are as lean as copper cables. I glance at the rams on the walls that watch over us like judges at a trial. Johnny brings me back to the conversation with one direct look.

'Okay, Ralph and Leila, was it?' Johnny's eyes aren't fighter's eyes, they're more like blue X-rays.

'Yeah, it was Leila,' I explain. 'But it's Lal now.' I'm named after my grandma, who everyone called Lil, so I had to become Lal.

Johnny Hart hovers a finger between us.

'You two, what? Married or somethin'?'

Ralph laughs. His eyes are happy and brown. He shakes his head as if Johnny's just told a joke.

'Not us.'

'Nah,' I say, 'just good friends.' I give Ralph a dirty look. 'Mostly, anyway.'

Johnny ignores my second joke. He seems like a person with a lot on his mind. Money, at a guess.

'I'm takin' two thousand sheep out on the road,' he says. 'The trip's gonna make me or break me.' His blue eyes are as hard and spiky as a handful of fencing staples. 'I need reliable people.'

I wait for more – there is no more. Then it becomes clear what he's driving at. He's waiting to see if we're prepared to say that we are the sort of people he wants, that we are these 'reliable' people. I also decide that it would mean absolutely zilch to him if we walked away. Tomorrow he wouldn't even remember we'd met.

'We can do it,' I say, plunging in. 'Can't we, Ralph? We work hard, don't we, mate? We're good workers.'

Ralph nods. 'Yeah, we are.' His nod is secretive, meaning that this Johnny Hart's got to prove himself to us just as much as we've got to prove ourselves to him. Fair enough, too. How

17

do we know he's as up-front as he's trying to make out? That he's actually got the dough for wages?

The shearer picks up his gear, slowly and carefully, a man used to carrying things – like my dad, who was in the removals business for thirty-five years.

'So, you in? One drover, one driver?' he asks. 'We could be out on the road for two months. No weekends off. Work straight through. Award wages, nothin' more, nothin' less.' He hasn't finished. 'It's gonna be hard and hot and dirty.' He adds more. 'Maybe dangerous, who knows? And not much fun. I don't mess 'round.'

Ralph and I swap a look. The eyes have it. Yeah, we're in. Up to our necks by the sound of it – but times are tough.

# three

The three of us pile into an ancient black Dodge utility that'd be at least forty years old. It sits with other cars and utes like a big-bottomed grandma amongst a bunch of quick, slick grandkids.

'Top bus,' I say, patting faded red upholstery that's shiny-grimy. 'An oldie but a goldie.' I breathe in the old car smell of oily rags, lost Fantales, and the evaporated mist of five thousand long-gone sandwiches, pies and cups of coffee. And the smell of Johnny Hart, too: dried perspiration, new flannel shirt, tea on his breath.

'She's a workhorse, all right.' The shearer fires her up, pushing the long floor shift into first. 'You could drive her, then?'

'Love to.'

We rumble towards the showgrounds gate, about to set sail for Johnny's place at Barramah. I've heard of Barramah; it's south-west of here somewhere, over the Queensland border and into New South Wales. Barramah. Not a big joint, that's for sure. And maybe not even small. Try tiny.

I turn, looking out the rear window. Rising above Carmen's

Games of Chance and the Frontier Shooting Gallery is the pointed top of Barley's Travelling Outback Boxing Show. I guess forever I'll be able to picture Danny Barley's boys fighting for their lives, letting it rip, smiling through split lips, toughing out every three-minute round.

Ralph watches Barley's tent sink into the mass of lonely small-town lights.

'Geez, perhaps I shoulda stuck – '

I knock his arm. 'Too late, mate. Onwards and upwards.'

In moments we're out of town, driving in silence through blackness. There's a funny old radio, but I'm not game to ask Johnny to turn it on. Ralph stares out at the patched road that slides at us as if drawn into the headlights.

It seems fighting's the hardest thing for a fighter to give up, even after losing – perhaps especially after losing. A lot goes on in a boxer's head that only another boxer could understand. I guess we've all got what we think are good reasons for doing what we do, or don't do.

'Hundred and fifty klicks to my joint,' Johnny says. 'I'll see if I can get the heater goin'.'

Good thinking. Around the border here it's not exactly as warm as the Gold Coast.


Ralph nods at a paddock drifting by us, the edge of it lit by the Dodge's pale lights.

'See the 'roos?'

A bunch of kangaroos stand like stark grey puppets, front paws hanging. The ground, as flat as a stage, looks hard and dry.

'Not much feed for 'em,' I venture, as the kangaroos are replaced by silvery gum trees shaped like wishbones.

'Forget the flaming 'roos,' says Johnny. 'At least they can get to what grass there is, which is more than the sheep can do. Which is one of the reasons why we're droving. To get to it too.' He eases his left leg, the one with the caliper on it, and leaves his round-knuckled fist sitting on faded work trousers.

'What are the other reasons?' I ask daringly.

Wrinkles pile up near Johnny's eyes. He toe-pokes the headlights down to low beam as a truck looms then blunders past. Johnny again lets the utility have the middle of the road.

'Main reason, if a bloke shoots his sheep, the government'll give him $1.80 a head. So instead of me takin' a cheque I was owed for shearing – ' He takes a sniff of chilly night air. 'I bought skinny sheep. Cheap.' He never takes his eyes off the road. 'So we go where the grass is and hopefully get 'em to the point where they're worth more alive than dead. Then we bring 'em home after it's rained. Hopefully.'

I'm confused. 'Who's paying who to shoot sheep?'

Johnny drives on unhurriedly, ten kilometres below the speed limit.

'Government pays the farmers. Someone's decided there's too many sheep. Reckon this is the way to get rid of a few, ah, million.'

Johnny pilots the Dodge over a rise and we sail downwards, between trees and shadows, white posts ticking past. Even at night I can tell the land is parched and hard up. I can smell dust, then the stink of rotting flesh as we pass and leave behind something dead.

'It's gotta rain soon,' Johnny says, his features not softened by the faint glow from the dashboard – a wide country face I can imagine sweat dripping off. 'Otherwise, plan B.'

'Which is?' I ask, being a great believer in plan Bs, and plan Cs too, come to that.

'Shoot the sheep and sell the farm.'

Nobody says anything. Ralph sits beside me, elbow rudely into my ribs, his boots on top of rope and a torn newspaper. Stubbornly the bull-nosed old Dodge pushes on, Moree somewhere behind us as we head south-west, staying out where it's dry, where the sheep huddle as if they're in the holding paddock of an abattoir. Not the most hopeful place in the world, I think, to make a last stand.

Johnny eases the black Dodge through the tin-roofed town of Barramah. Fifteen seconds worth of shops, pub, and one war memorial. I can't remember ever seeing it on any map – and now I know why.

The boss clicks on the indicator, slows down, and we judder over a cattle grid and into a property. 'Barramah Downs' announces a flaking sign on a warped board. Spiky grass prods the underside of a rusting milk can that serves as a letterbox, and in the sweep of headlights I see a white cottage, tin sheds, and a hill swelling up behind like a wave.

We stop behind the small weatherboard house to be met by the harsh sounds of barking dogs and rattling chains. An outside light is on as a woman empties a teapot onto a scraggly garden. Johnny kills the motor.

'G'day,' he calls out into the darkness. The woman lifts a hand but doesn't come near the car, although she must be able to see Ralph and me in it. She stares briefly, then walks back up the broken path.

'Dell,' says Johnny Hart, turning. 'My sister. We run the place.' He pushes open the door, not taking the keys from the ignition. The seat lifts as he slides out. 'Back in a tick.' He follows his sister into the lit-up kitchen.

Ralph and I get out of the ute, which I've christened Black Betty, and stand and stretch, trying to see what we can see.

There's a home-made clothes-line propped on sticks, two identical white dresses hanging off it and half a dozen pairs of patched work pants. In a paddock I can make out a few horses under a dusty cypress tree.

'There's your horses, mate. I hope you weren't kidding when you said you could ride one.'

'Same here.' Ralphy stands with his hands up in between his singlet and cloth shirt. He looks tired, knocked around.

Further up the track I see a hayshed leaning into a wind that isn't blowing and rusty farm machinery resting in long grass – and I wonder how I always manage to find myself in places where life's a battle. Around here I'd say things are tough, that Johnny and his sister are doing it hard, and that there's a fair chance of everything collapsing into one awfully flat heap. No wonder they don't talk much. It's probably better than giving or getting nothing else but bad news. And I know.

When my old man's removals business was about to go under, he said about four words in four months. And they were, 'it's bloody had it'. And I'd say, looking around, that this outfit's pretty close to going the same way.

We're eating chops, mashed potatoes, peas, and carrots, and we're using old cutlery with handles faded to a buttery yellow.

Johnny's sister Dell mustn't be all that hungry. She sits elbows on the table, most of her meal untouched, and studies Ralph and me. I noticed before she's wearing two beautiful old rings, but not on her wedding finger. The rings suit her; sapphires and rubies so old they don't sparkle, and plain gold bands. I doubt she'd ever wear anything that would sparkle at all. This Dell's not what I'd call old, say thirty-seven, thirty-eight, but she's not going out of her way to act all that young, either.

'What d'you think of this droving idea?' she asks me. 'Of taking two thousand starving sheep and trying to fatten 'em up out in the backblocks? Any thoughts?' She forks up a quarter of potato.

Johnny and his sister certainly aren't beat-about-the-bush types. My folks always told us that to make a guest feel uncomfortable was pretty rude. And that staring was a no-no, and so were elbows on the table. Dell's just blown the lot.

'Sounds fair enough,' I say uneasily. 'Johnny says there's grass out there for them to eat and it's probably gonna rain.' I pour tomato sauce, home-made, onto my potatoes. God, what do I know about sheep? At home all we had was a ginger cat called Ratty, a budgie, and Timmy the three-legged dog.

Dell takes a swatch of straight black hair and flicks it back with a well-used hand. Dark skin under her eyes makes her look tired. She's good-looking, though; her cheekbones slant up and her mouth is even and wide, but she seems to have forgotten all about her looks. Worrying about money tends to do that to a person.

'So there's grass out there, Lal, and it's going to rain.'

I just said that, didn't I? I look at Ralph, who looks at his plate.

'Well, I hope it's going to rain,' I add, thinking these questions from Dell might be intended for Johnny equally as much as they're intended for me.

Johnny leans back, leaving his knife and fork in the middle of his empty plate.

'Drop it, Dell. Getting narky never pushed up the wool price or brought on a thunderstorm.'

I doubt Dell would drop anything just because someone asked her to; but she does, and goes back to stabbing baby carrots.

'No one should shoot good sheep,' says Ralph slowly and clearly. 'Not if they don't have to.'

A forkful of food stops short of my mouth. I force it to go all the way, then chew on it as if it was blotting paper. This statement is actually not out of character for Ralph. For half an hour he won't say a word, then he'll state his case in front of anyone at any time. Which can be dangerous, but good luck to him anyhow.

'No one wants to shoot sheep,' Johnny says eventually. 'What Dell's driving at is that she reckons I shouldn't have bought the sheep in the first place.'

Ralph nods, his skin looking velvety in the bright kitchen light. His face is wide, well proportioned, kind of classical; apart from his nose, which has been hammered off-centre.

'Why did you then? Buy 'em?'

'To stock this place,' says Johnny. 'And because I had the dough, and because the sheep are that bloody good I'd never be able to afford 'em like that again. Ever, not at the price I got 'em. Skinny as they are.'

'Even if we do end up having to shoot them,' says Dell, and pushes her plate to one side. 'But so long as it rains, so long as the wool price goes up, and so long as we can afford to drove them, we'll be right. But – ' A vague smile, not happy, plucks up the corners of her mouth. 'But we've got them now, so that's that, I guess. You guys can do the dishes.' She gets up and walks out through the back screen door. A few moments later cigarette smoke drifts back through the wire to itch in my nose.

Johnny breaks the silence.

'That's what we're up against.' He allows us to see the crack of a smile. 'Not Dell, but every other thing. I told you fellas it's not gonna be easy. It's a long shot. D'you see the horses, Ralph?'

'Yeah,' says Ralph, 'they look all right. Not too wild.'

Johnny stacks plates. 'Got no use for wild horses. They gotta do the job like everybody else.'

I decide Johnny Hart's okay. His sister Dell I'm not so sure about. I guess she's trying to suss us out in five minutes flat, see what we're like and what we think.

'Where'd you say you're from, Ralph?' Johnny collects cutlery as if he was gathering kindling. 'What kinda things've you been doing?'

Ralph's hands crab awkwardly on the plastic tablecloth, then he tucks them into his armpits.

'I come from Echuca. On the Murray. I was workin' at the sawmill down there for a while. Before that I was pickin' fruit at Shepparton.' He looks at a bench where dead flowers wait to be thrown out. 'I did a bit of fightin' down Melbourne and up Bendigo,' he adds. 'For money. Then I left home – for a holiday. Then I joined the boxin' tent.'

Left Echuca for a holiday? I let that one ride. It's his story, I guess he can tell it how he likes.

Johnny returns to the table, bringing a white plastic ice-cream container with him.

'How about you, Lal?' He gives me the full benefit of his unavoidable eyes.

'Well,' I say, 'I come from a joint on the New South Wales south coast called Delaney Bay. It's pretty small. And after I quit school I did five months at the Sea Free Tuna canning factory at Bermagui, which wasn't too bad.' Not too bad, if you like putting dead fish in tin cans, that is. 'Then I was on the dole, then I got a pub job in Goondiwindi.' I go on a bit about wanting to travel and see some stuff. 'Then I somehow got talked into joining Barley's boxing tent. The rest's history.'

I still don't know how that slippery dude, Danny Barley,

managed to talk me out from behind the public bar and into joining his show. Maybe I had an idea the boxing tent was something out of the ordinary; that maybe it was something I could write a story about, for a newspaper or something. Start of my career! That was one dumb idea that flashed through my head a while back. I like the idea of stories. I reckon some of the things I see would make really good ones – it's just that when I put them in my diary they sound absolutely putrid.

Dell's come back inside and sits next to me, smelling of stale smoke.

'Did Johnny tell you about Kate?' she asks, sliding a green plastic lighter towards an empty glass vase.

'Nope,' I say. 'Is she a drover?' I was going to say, is she a drover's dog – but wisely decide against it.

A piece of the steel edging comes off the table. Johnny belts it back on with the heel of his hand.

'Nup, she's at uni. She's coming with us, though, to help out.' He opens one hand as if freeing information. 'She's the daughter of my old man's brother's son, whatever that makes her. You work it out. I've rung her, now that I've got you two. She'll be here tomorrow. She's taken this year off from study, so she's offered her services. She's a good kid.'

'What's she studying?' I ask, interested, because sometimes I kind of wish I'd done some more studying myself – not a hard conclusion to come to when you're faced with a lifetime of tinning tuna or pulling beers.

'Law,' says Dell, taking over the conversation. 'She's done two years at Sydney Uni.' Dell fiddles with her cigarettes. 'She's got a horse and she loves to ride. She's spent a fair bit of time up here and on other properties. She likes it, for some reason, considering she's from town.'

'Her family live in Mosman,' Johnny adds. 'You can see the old ferries from the kitchen window.'

All I know about Sydney is that if you can see the water from the kitchen sink, you're loaded. So where d'you keep a horse in Mosman? In a boatshed?

'How come she took a year off from uni?' Ralph asks. 'Doesn't she like it? Isn't she doing real well?'

Johnny gives the white ice-cream container an idle spin. Written on it in black letters is the word Chooks.

'Oh, she's doing all right. She always does. She just wanted to do a few different things, see a few things. She's always been shooting off to various places, travelling. Like you and Lal.'

Well, not exactly like Ralph and Lal, not at all when you think about it. I bet this Kate gets to choose the places she sees and the things she does, whereas Ralph and I get blown around like a couple of grass seeds at the mercy of all four winds.

Well, good luck to her. One day I hope Ralphy and I'll be able to pick our own directions, too.

# four

My morning's work is to clean the old Dodge ute inside and out, whilst Ralph helps Johnny shoe the horses. This I do, ending up with a dollar's worth of dirty coins, half a bale of rotting hay, a handful of old shopping lists, six pens that don't work, and a sweaty forehead. Enough. I take a breather, leaning on Bett's nicely rounded front mudguard, and watch a white utility and horse float drag a plume of dust from the road to the house. I presume this is Kate Hart.

The utility stops and a girl, easily taller than me – as tall as Ralph – gets out. She's got thick, fair, expensive-looking hair pulled back into a long ponytail and her jeans are snagged up over the backs of brown riding boots. She stretches, tucks in her navy blue shirt, then looks around for signs of life. I guess that's my cue.

I wipe my paws on a rag then wander towards the house. Dried leaves rattle in a dead vegetable garden, a spot of grease on the end of my nose doesn't help by tending to make me go cross-eyed.

'Gidday,' I call out as I close in. 'You must be Kate.' In the hot air my voice sounds as loud and gritty as a parrot's.

Kate's main priority seems to be her nose. It's red and sore-looking. I bet it's flaky around the edges. She blows it on a big white hanky that's wet enough to be see-through.

'Yeah, Kate Hart,' she says, stuffing the hanky down into her jeans pocket. 'And I hate my nose. Hayfever.' Her eyes, as blue as her shirt, leak silvery little tears in the corners.

I stick out my hand to shake. Kate Hart extends hers slowly.

'It's wet,' she says. 'I'm warning you.'

'Mine's greasy,' I answer. We shake. She's right, hers is wet. I turn a groan into a giggle.

'I'm Lal Godwin. I'll be drivin' the ute. It's a beauty. I love it already.'

Kate puts on a creamy wide-brimmed hat. It looks new. Her boots are old, though, but they're as shiny as acorns kept in a kid's pocket. My boots, bought a month ago, have yet to encounter polish in their short, hard life. And look like it.

'Johnny mentioned you on the phone,' says Kate. 'How's it all going? There'd be a fair bit to get organised, I imagine?'

Her voice is definitely a city voice. It has a smooth, sure tone to it; like I bet she orders Chinese food by name and not by number. Matches her perfectly; like the plaited bush belt matches her flat-heeled boots.

'Nothing we can't handle,' I say carefully. I jiggle my thumb in the direction of the hill. 'Johnny's up with Ralph shoeing the horses and Dell's in town buying stuff. Where'd you drive from? Sydney?'

'No, Tamworth.' Kate turns abruptly. 'I've got a few uni friends there.' She makes her way around to the back of the horse float.

I follow, a few steps behind. I'm not real keen on horses.

They're large enough to do you serious damage. Kate lowers the rear ramp. For a city person she seems pretty sure about all this country stuff. Without a backward glance she steps straight into the float with what looks like a very big, very black nag. Somehow she must have noted the pained look on my face.

'What's the problem, Lal?' she asks across a broad, rounded bare back. 'Don't you like horses? Can't you ride?'

'Both,' I say and move no closer. 'That's why I'll be driving the ute.'

The horse, shiny in the sun, backs awkwardly down the bending ramp. Once it's on flat earth Kate rubs its long black face and rearranges its mane like a mother fussing over a kid's fringe. Horses have very big heads, I just realised.

'This is Massy. Short for Massive.' Kate keeps working at the mane with long, strong fingers. 'You'll have to learn to ride, Lal. If we're droving you've got to be able to sit on a horse. I'll teach you. It's not that hard.' She pats the horse with her flat hand, making a sound like a thong slapping wet concrete.

Suddenly all this is a bit much for me. What with chooks cackling, the sun beating down on my shorn and hatless head, and Kate who seems to have everything well under control, I need a break.

'I'm puttin' the kettle on,' I say. 'Why don't you stick that horse somewhere safe, then go and get Ralph and Johnny?'

'Sure.' Kate clips a rope onto the horse's halter and starts to tow it towards the sheds. 'See you in ten minutes.' Kate has a watch on, too. A man's watch by the look of it, flat and big, with a blue and red strap.

I watch her walk away, unswayed by the swaying horse. She ambles casually, her free hand swinging as if she was brushing the tops of flowers. I guess she seems nice enough, in a smoothly-finished North Shore sort of a way.

I go in through the screen door, put on the kettle, and sit at the table with my chin on my hand. I don't feel so good.

Whenever I meet people like Kate my confidence slides. It's not just the money or the clothes, it's something else – it's the sheer easiness that people like her do stuff. The world seems to be their oyster, complete with pearl. They make me feel dumb, plain, and noisy. And rough. Look at my stupid haircut and all my dumb earrings. Look at my broken nails, pale skin, and gingery freckles. Look at my tuna-factory job, my bombing out of school – then look at their uni courses, cars, complexions, their . . . everything! Goddamn.

I tell myself to stop being such a wuss. I'm okay. Mostly I am anyway. I'm all right. I bloody am.


After morning tea I go up to the paddock to see how a horseshoe is put on a horse. From where I stand it appears quite scientific. Johnny lifts the horse's foot, slaps a horseshoe on it, then belts big silver nails into it with a hammer. I poke Ralph with a finger.

'How d'you know that doesn't hurt 'em, Ralph?'

He wipes his nose with the back of a hand.

'Because the boss says so, Lal.' He winks slyly. 'And after this, we're gonna file old Charlie's teeth. And that won't hurt him, either.'

I study a stroppy-looking chestnut horse that Johnny is currently assaulting with a hammer.

'I don't think I'd talk so loud, mate.'

Ralph laughs, his cheap black cowboy hat pulled down to his black eyebrows. Faded jeans pile up around his riding boots. He looks at Kate.

'He's a nice-lookin' horse that one of yours, eh? Big. Strong. Good-lookin' fella.'

Kate nods. She's so neat, even though she's not so small. Where my jeans are a little too baggy in places, hers are a little too tight. But everything she has on looks so well-washed, ironed, polished and matched I'd wear it to a nightclub. Except maybe the watch. Kate looks at her horse, who's slurping water from an old white bath near the fence.

'Yeah, but he's not exactly a stockhorse – ' She produces her hanky and blows her nose. 'I'm training him to be an eventing horse. But he's not quite there yet, and neither am I.'

I don't ask her what an eventing horse is. Maybe it's a horse you only take to big events, like the Olympic Games?

'He won't mind just plodding along, though,' Kate adds, looking at him affectionately. 'Get a bit of the fat off him. And me.' She slaps her hip.

Fat? If Kate's fat my sister Nadine's a hippopotamus. Kate's not fat, she's built like the tourist girls I used to see jogging dead slowly along Delaney Bay's surf beach at sunset; well-fed maybe, kind of curvy sure, but not fat. A grasshopper pings away from Kate's boot as she scuffs at a tuft of grass.

'Feed's a bit thin on the ground.' Her ponytail swings. 'It's bad just about all the way to Sydney.'

'I'd believe it.' Johnny drives a final nail, then points with the hammer. 'Swap us this for that file, would you, Lal?'

I hand him a long grey file, then I leave them to it. Watch dentistry like that without a needle? You've got to be joking. I go back to loading a mountain of camping gear into the back of the ute. How come I get all the good jobs?

Dell asks me to help her feed the dogs. She drops boiled bones into a white tin bucket and points to a bag of dog cubes that smell like sawdust mixed with sawdust.

We walk up past the shearing shed, turn left into the sunset, and make our way down to two bent peppertrees that sigh in the breeze. Four dogs bark from outside hollow log kennels, chains scraping.

'Two cups of dried stuff and one bone,' Dell tells me. 'And don't worry, none of them bite.'

I kneel, keeping an eye on a kelpie who's keeping two caramel coloured eyes on me. 'Nice doggie,' I say, 'here's your beautiful dinner.'

Quite happily I manage to make house calls to three of the four dogs, but hesitate in front of the last.

'I don't know whether you've noticed, Dell,' I call out, 'but this dog ain't no sheepdog.' It's a Rottweiler.

Dell almost laughs. 'Satan? He's harmless.'

Timidly I fill Satan's dinted silver bowl, being careful not to make any movements that might indicate I want to be bitten.

'He ain't wagging his tail,' I yell over my shoulder. 'I'll tell you that much.'

Dell gives me a semi-dirty look, but seems to relax a bit.

'The magpie-coloured one is Tiger,' she informs me. 'The big kelpie is Rowan, and the little kelpie's Jeannie, because she's a bloody genius of a dog.'

Jeannie has fur the colour of chocolate cake and eyes that gaze inquiringly. She wags her tail carefully, as if she thinks it might come off.

'The other dogs are good,' Dell says, 'but Jeannie's brilliant. Best dog Glen or Johnny ever had.'

Who's Glen? The rings on her hand? I don't ask.

I kneel next to the lightweight kelpie and pat her lightly on the head.

'So what's a nice girl like you living in a hollow log like this, eh?' Her ears, which are like a pair of junior-sized party hats, flicker. She puts her head to one side then presses a cool nose into my hand. 'You're a good dog,' I tell her.

'She's a good worker,' Dell says. 'She's a $2000 dog. A career girl of the canine world.'

Dogs I trust a lot more than horses.

'Why've you got Satan?' I ask. 'Lions?'

Dell laughs, which is a first.

'No, Glen bought him as a guard dog for me when he and Johnny were off shearing. Glen was my husband. He and Johnny always worked together. They bought this place together, too.' She looks at me. 'With my help.'

There. I thought there was something like that with her. I figured she might've been married. I decide it'd be safer to talk about Satan the guard dog, and not her husband.

'He's got a good set of choppers, old Satan,' I say. 'And nice eyes.'

For a few moments we listen to the soft jingle-jangle of dog chains in the dust and the feathery brushing of the pep-pertrees. A magpie warbles, a sound pure and soft, like shallow water running down between pebbles. So, where is this hus-band, then?

Dell pushes her hair around, then puts the tips of her fin-gers into the tops of her jean pockets.

'After Glen was killed,' she says, 'Satan didn't have a clue. Took him months to realise that Glen wasn't going to come back.' Dell picks up the empty white bucket. 'For a while there whenever I looked at the mutt, or he looked at me, I'd burst into tears.' She glances at the dog as stony eyed as if she's never cried in her life. 'Hard to believe how quick things can change.'

I think I know what she means. When my friend Indi Em died, the world stopped, and I'm not joking. For weeks I did nothing but sit or walk on the beach. I couldn't even listen to music, or go bodyboarding. Indi had some complicated blood disease, and in the last few weeks she faded like a flower until she seemed small enough to drift away. Then in front of my eyes she did. Em and I had plans – to do things, write stuff, travel, be famous – yeah, sure. Two years ago she died and I haven't recovered yet.

'My best friend died,' I say carefully, 'and kind of all I had left were all these questions. Like, how unfair is this? And why? And no one could tell me – anything.' I pick up the sack of dog cubes.

Shadows, long and low, lie over stark stubbly paddocks. Sadness floats, whether it comes from the land or from Dell, or from me I don't know, but I can feel it. I can even put a colour to it; it's mauve, like lavender, or mauve like the hills I can see way way away. And it's cold.

The chipped white bucket lifts as Dell talks, bright against her jeans.

'Glen's idea was to get this place up and running as a real sheep property.' She looks at the rag-tag fences, the sheep packed around a single trough in the distance. 'But I don't know if we can do it. I don't know if it can be done. The place is even further away from being any good than it ever was. For Johnny to buy those sheep now. God, we argued over that. If we lose them, we're gone.'

The bare, eroded paddocks back up Dell's words. She's no wishful thinker, that's for sure; she's not scared to state or face facts. I doubt she's a quitter, though.

'We'll bring 'em back fat,' I say. 'I promise.'

'I hope so.' Dell stands with the bucket, belonging absolutely to this place. 'But it's not that simple. If Glen was here he'd – ' She stops, like a train in a siding, as if it's simply not possible for her to go any further.

We leave the dogs and walk past the shearing shed, hearing it rattle and groan as the wind ducks in under loose tin sheets. I know Dell won't say any more. And neither will I, figuring we've come to the end of what we're capable of telling each other, for today anyway.

I wish she was coming with us, but she's not. She works as a sister at the local hospital. I think her wages are going towards paying ours. Hell, I hope it rains, and soon.

We – me, Ralph, Kate, Dell and Johnny – sit around the kitchen table and eat canned peaches, which I opened.

'I used to work at a canning factory,' I say to everyone, spooning up half a slushy slice of peach. 'Not peaches, but. Tuna. It was hell, 'specially for the fish.'

Ralph and Kate laugh. Perhaps Johnny and Dell didn't hear me?

'I said it was hell, 'specially for the – ' No, perhaps they did.

'My worst job was selling ties in David Jones,' says Kate. 'Because one day I decided that ties are about the silliest thing anybody could wear. I mean, what use are they, really?'

'No use,' says Ralph. 'They strangle you.'

'Bowties are worse,' I add, and slice a peach with the side of my spoon. 'Only a bozo would wear a bowtie. Or a clown.' I can't remember the last time I ate canned peaches. I'd forgotten how good and gooey they are.

'My dad wears bowties sometimes,' says Kate. 'Big ones. And braces. He's in a fashion zone all of his own. He's kind of eccentric, actually.'

Gulp. Foot in gob.

'He's a doctor,' she adds, telling me. 'I'm sure people laugh at him. We give him the worst ties and the widest braces we can find. He wears them all. He forgets he has them on. He's vague. It runs in the family.'

It seems Dell isn't interested in ties, bowties, braces, or vagueness. She asks Kate what her parents think of her taking a year off from uni.

Kate pushes her empty, creamy bowl out in front of her. I must say, she does seem to like to eat.

'Dad's not so bad.' Kate rubs a dot of cream off her shirt with the corner of her hanky. 'But my mum's not impressed. She thinks I should finish the degree before I do anything else at all. She thinks I'll never go back now.'

'But you will, won't you?' I ask. 'I mean, if you've already done two years . . .'

'I don't know if I want to be a lawyer,' Kate says straightforwardly. 'It sounds glamorous, but – '

'Lots of dough,' says Ralph quietly, 'wouldn't it be?'

Kate shrugs as if money was something she was used to trying not to talk about.

'Yes, I suppose.' She studies the plastic salt and pepper shakers. 'But lots of time as well. You wouldn't have time to do anything else, and I do want to do other things.' She picks up her spoon and delicately licks it. 'I want to keep riding, travel, maybe I'll try and write a book or something, who knows? I want to – '

'A book?' I say, and see that Johnny and Dell seem as impressed with book talk as they were with bowties.

Maybe Johnny and Dell are like my folks, who think books are a waste of time and paper? In fact, I'm the only Godwin who's ever read a book. Godwins generally read magazines. I read *Rolling Stone*, my sister reads anything with a supermodel on the front of it, Mum reads the *Weekly*, Laurie reads car mags, and Dad reads about how to put innocent worms on very sharp hooks.

'I've got a diary,' I put in, 'it's dreadful, but it's good to

write down stuff every now and again, so you don't forget.'
That of course isn't the reason I do it, but it sounds as if it
could be. I guess I keep my diary because at school Miss
Bateman once said I was a 'good journalist'. This was
probably just a nice way to say that I didn't have any
imagination.

We finish tea quietly. Forget books. Forget school. Forget
law careers. Forget home. They won't make rain or save sheep.
Tomorrow we leave, for weeks or maybe months on the road,
a motley crew if ever there was one. Apart from Kate, of
course.

After tea I go to my room and I do dig out my diary. Today
would be a good day to make a fresh start. I leave a buffer
zone of ten empty pages.

*7th March*

*Barramah Downs, Barramah. North-east New South Wales.*
*Weather: hot and cloudy.*

*I guess this trip will be character building, if nothing else. It will be if I'm
missing out on showers. Ralphy seems toey, but is okay. He's keeping
everything close to his chest. I know he'll be trying his hardest to do a
good job. I hope Johnny can see this. I hope Johnny isn't the kind of boss
who hands out the orders like some Nazi and won't give an inch.*

*Kate Hart is the eldest of three girls, she informs me. She's got sisters called
Eliza and Lauren. Sound like the royal family. She learnt to ride when
she was three on a pony called Podgy. The white utility is hers, but the
horse float is borrowed. Perhaps she's not quite as loaded as I first
thought. She still lives at home, too. Their house is big, she says, but
shabby . . . yeah, I bet. They inherited it from grandpa. Score! All we*

ever inherited was Ratty the cat from the people next door. Come to think of it, he's pretty shabby, too.

Dell Hart is okay. I think I understand her better, now that I know about her husband getting killed. Maybe you never get over something like that? As I said, after Indi Emma Jane died everything around me lost its colour. It wasn't as if I didn't want to do things, I just couldn't. Least of all schoolwork. So I dropped out, which was on the cards anyway.

So, tomorrow we begin to make a piece of Australian history. Things'll happen, that's for sure. And my dad'll be interested. He likes all that old Banjo Paterson stuff. He's got the record! Bet Kate's family have got the book. Told you us Godwins are a primitive bunch.

# five

I imagine that when drovers set off on a long drive they move out quietly, steely eyes scanning the horizon – but not us. We head out with twenty-five cheering neighbours scaring the daylights out of the horses, and some idiot blaring the theme from *Rocky* – da da dah! du du duh! – from a utility filled with large country lads who've obviously all eaten their Weeties, and a few stubbies, for breakfast. One of them with a big, round, jolly moon-face, and a blue shirt untucked, bounds up to the Dodge's window and pokes in a rather too fresh rabbit's foot.

'This is for good luck, Spike,' he says, then kisses me smack! on the cheek. 'Carn,' he adds charmingly, 'give us a real one! Open up. Pretend I'm a bigtime Tamworth Country 'n Western singin' star.'

I put Bett into first. 'In your dreams, cloth-head.' Then I drive off, although the big idiot's still half in the window.

He falls out. These country dudes are unbreakable anyway. I look for Ralph and see him riding on a small horse the colour of a dirty white egg. Ralphy doesn't exactly look relaxed, but even from here I can tell he's half happy. And half worried.

There is, I reckon, a heroic buzz in the air. These skinny sheep straight from death row, a boss trying to save their woolly souls, and learner drovers trying to learn something. The colours and sounds hit me right in the heart.

Sky. Dust. Sheep. Horses. Hats. Wire. So what if I'm getting carried away? Maybe this is what I want – to be part of something big, brave and maybe brilliant. Blood, sweat and tears? Probably, but nothing ventured, nothing gained or sprained. Something like that.

A family waving a green boxing-kangaroo flag flags me down. I stop the Dodge. The woman, small, skinny and sun-dried, hands over a shoe-box filled with biscuits wrapped in an ironed tea-towel.

'Here you go, love, for later on. Good luck. We hope it works out.' Her words are put forward like the biscuits, simply.

I thank her, thank them. The husband, as tall and strong-looking as a tree, releases a smile from amongst the crags of his face and the two boys, looking like mushrooms in big brown hats, yell like mad. Then fight over who's going to wave the flag.

'The kids'll be praying for yers,' the woman informs me cheerfully. 'I'll make 'em.' She steps forward to bend down to the window. 'Got all your feminine requirements, have yer? Cause out there – '

'I have,' I say, and suddenly this simple down-to-earth concern begins to upset my emotional applecart. Kindness from a stranger. One thing money can't buy.

Another of Johnny's neighbours insists we take two of his dogs – known as Dusty-dog and Dirty-dog – and after a short growling match with our trio, they set off steadily, scouting the sheep. I drive on, but stop a short way down the road where I uncap my wee camera, and start snapping as two thousand merino ewes spread out into the roadside grass. There are horses, riders, kelpies and border collies, and every sheep bleats as if it is off for a day at the Royal Easter Show.

Suddenly it strikes me that I'm truly a part of all this; that I'm here because I've got things to do, duties to perform, and people are relying on me. That would explain why I've got a nervy, happy feeling in my stomach, a map folded on the dashboard, and a huge pile of camping gear in the back.

'We're goin',' I yell. 'This is gonna be big!'

And we are going, Bett's black bonnet is aimed downhill, I give a last long-distance wave to Dell, then I resolve to look only forwards. When a drover and her truck are out in the legendary 'long paddock', it's eyes on the road, hands on the wheel, and a hope in my heart that Aileen, the grey horse in the float, will not rock the boat whatsoever.

Bett's easy to drive, although with the float on behind she doesn't exactly handle like a Formula One racing car – but I'm getting used to her sedate style of forward motion. And because we're going about twenty-five kilometres an hour tops, I'm hoping that I'll end up nowhere near that famous creek where no one goes swimming and paddles are in short supply.

So I'm driving carefully, because if I prang there's half a tonne of gear that couldn't be replaced, and a horse that'll hold me responsible. Old-timer gum trees nod at me politely as Bett and I pass, keeping us company and on the straight and narrow track. In three kilometres I'm to stop at Sawcut Creek where I'll set up camp and get the tucker ready. The others'll catch me up later this afternoon, and although I think maybe I got the rough end of the workload stick, it's better to have one end of the stick than no end at all.

The last thing I want is horse trouble. So what do I run into as soon as I try to persuade Aileen, supposedly the quietest horse of the lot, to leave the float? An animal with attitude. Will she back down the ramp? Does she even look like she might? No way. All she does is stand there, eyes forward, ears back, and snorts at me whenever I gather the courage to actually get inside the float with her.

'Okay then, cobber,' I tell her. 'Stay there. See if I care. I've got work to do.'

I off-load swags into a sea of silvery grass and undernourished trees. I light a cooking fire and stockpile so much firewood I feel like a millionaire. Then I go back to the monster and lob a few words at the back of her head.

'Getting hot in there, Aileen?' No answer. 'It's cooler out here.' Nothing.

In through the narrow door at the front of the float I go, coming face to face with her long grey one. Gently I try to push her back down the ramp. She doesn't budge. Obviously I am not welcome in her own personal space. Obviously she also has a bit of mule in her. She's staying put. I give up and leave her there.

I don't believe it. Well, I do, but I don't how or why this has happened, somehow Aileen has taken herself out of the float and is now eating grass. I feel like kissing her.

Instead I cautiously capture the trailing end of the rope attached to her halter, then I stand in the one place as if she's a big kite that won't take off. Now what? Tie her up, I guess. That's on the list that Johnny gave me, written in red ink, with lots of underlining.

'Come on, dear.' I tug the rope. She ignores me, and continues her love affair with the grass.

I tug again, harder, to show who's boss. She is. She doesn't move a millimetre. I give up and tie her to a rail on the float. This way she can't run away, but she can keep on eating. I pat her neck a few times, then I go away, with the uneasy feeling I haven't made too much progress on the horse-handling aspect of my job. No need to tell the boss the full story, though, I don't think.

Preparing a drover's camp requires more than slinging around a few swags and bunging a few bangers on the barbie. Sure, bedding and dinner have to be handled, the spare horse has to be looked after, wood has to be collected, and water has to be heated – but most importantly the 'brake' has to be set up.

The brake is a temporary pen for the sheep made of rope netting and kept upright with wooden stakes. It also requires an expert to position it – this being the case I kick it off the back of Bett and leave it for Johnny.

I then set about wrapping spuds in foil, cleaning the grill, boiling water, and trying not to stress-out too much about getting everything exactly right.

Doing stuff right is big in my family. In fact, when times were tough, it probably kept us going. I can still see my dad, Ray, neatly folding the holey blankets and tie-downs he kept in the back of his removals truck, even though no one had hired him for days. And Mum watching him through the kitchen window, bringing him mugs of tea on the hour every hour. I guess they thought that once they stopped doing things as they'd always done them, everything'd fall to bits.

So I try hard too. Mostly. Who wants to be a failure? Nobody. I want Johnny to be pleased with me. I want him to see that I won't stack the ute or lose a bloody horse or start a bushfire. I'm sure he thinks a bloke could do the job better;

and maybe some outback fella could. But he ain't got one, he's got me, and I'm not as dumb as I look, despite what my school reports said. Neither is Ralph. Sure, we're not lawyers like Kate, but we're not second-class citizens either.

And now we've got our chance to prove it too. Which I guess is all anyone can ever ask for.

In the distance I can hear the mob. The sheep maa! And baa! Dogs bark, voices leap back and forth. I check the camp, cover everything that the flies fancy, and walk out onto the track. The sweat dries as I move, cooling my forehead and under my arms.

One of my dad's favourite movies is *The Sundowners*, a real old black-and-white and fuzzy thing. The sundowners were drovers and had silly accents – but now that movie seems better than I thought it was. Droving's like a long voyage, even if it is taken at walking pace on dry, dry land. Johnny's made us all that extra bit watchful because you're at the mercy of the weather and anything else that can affect the sheep.

I watch the flock pushing along the hard-baked road, wobbling through grey-blue heat haze. An eroded creek as wide as a river winds down a scorched hill. It's hard to believe that three hundred or four hundred kilometres beyond is Coffs Harbour, as the crow flies – but none do around here. They sit in dead trees like little black witches and watch us pass.

The first rider I can make out is Ralph, cut-off shirt showing brown arms, reins held neatly in one hand. He waves slowly, tiredly. He looks exhausted, on the horse that plods, head low, one hoof breaking the crusty dirt after the other. Ralph and I walk in front of the mob.

'Good day?' I ask. 'No stuff-ups? Didn't fall off? Get bitten by a snake?'

Ralph pulls a long brown grass-seed from a blue and white footy sock and flicks it away.

'Yeah, it was okay. Johnny told me to shut up, but.' He looks back over the slowly moving flock. 'I was calling the dogs and it was confusin' 'em, he reckons.' Ralph shakes his head. 'He reckons they've gotta get used to me. Reckons I don't know enough about it to work 'em properly.'

I slap Ralph's dusty boot. I tell him not to worry about it.

'Look, this stuff ain't easy, mate. We're only beginners. We'll get on top of it, eh? How was Kate?'

Ralph looks for her, spots her along the fence line on her big black horse.

'Yeah, she's okay. She didn't say much, but lent me her Aeroguard and a rubber-band thing for me hair. She's a good rider.'

There's a shout from behind. Johnny rides up to us on the chestnut stockhorse called Charlie.

'Everythin' all right?' He holds a coiled whip, his face is stubbly, and with his calipered leg he looks a bit like Mad Max. 'What's the problem?'

'No problem,' I say. Unlike some bosses, Johnny doesn't bother trying to sound like he isn't one. 'Camp's set up,' I tell him. 'Fire's going. Dinner's organised. Just come to see the sheep.'

His hat moves, a shadow slides down his shirt.

'Okay, you seen 'em. Go back and I'll be there in a few minutes. The mob'll stop here until you an' me have got the brake up, so get goin'. And be careful about leavin' the fire.'

I get.


Johnny rides into camp, pulling up on Charlie, then slides off the horse as easily as I could fall off a log.

'Grab the sledge hammer.' He looks at the rolled-up brake on the ground. 'What's it doin' down there?'

'Not a lot,' I say.

'It stays in the back of the ute,' he informs me. 'So you and I don't have to carry the thing all around the bloody country-side.'

That makes sense.

'I'll get it right tomorrow.' I manage to stop myself saying 'sir'.

We lift the brake back into Bett, then drive a short way cross-country, stopping where we can make use of a farmer's fence.

I'm sent back to get the hammer, which I left on the ground. Off I go, feeling like a ninny. When I get tired I get forgetful and do really stupid things. Like tearing my shirt on the barbed wire.

'Ah shit!'

Johnny doesn't say a word. He unrolls the brake then starts to set it up panel by panel in a rough semicircle, me sweating like a pig because the hammer's so heavy, but I keep banging away until the boss tries to take it off me.

'Nah,' I say, 'I can do it.'

'Yeah, but I can do it better.'

I hand it over. 'Get me a smaller one for Christmas.' If that comment breaks any ice, I fail to see any cubes.

The brake is up, surrounding grey dirt and gold grass. Over the fence I can make out the remains of a railway line; no rails, no sleepers, only a scrubby embankment arrowing off across yellow paddocks. I ask Johnny where it used to go. He props his boot on a bare log, hand clamped on his thigh.

'Connected with the line to Narrabri. Built by diggers come back from the First World War. From one tough thing to another, eh?'

'You can say that again,' I say, looking at the old line, picturing a work gang in flannel singlets toiling as slowly as ants across the ground, slaving away with picks **and s**hovels.

I look at the line and I wonder what those guys talked about, say at morning smoko or around the fire at night, with the war behind them and the future right in front of them – being another long hot day of hard yakka. I wish I could walk along that line and think myself back all those years. I like thinking about the type of place Australia has been and the types of people who've been here. Time is funny stuff. You don't remember it passing, then suddenly it has, and things have changed.

Johnny and I go to meet the sheep, his caliper marking time with small leathery slaps as we walk. He doesn't talk. Neither do I, although talking is one thing I do a lot of. Too much, I've been told.

We sit around the fire drinking coffee and eating chocolate. Kate drinks herbal tea to control her hayfever. It doesn't work. It's seven o'clock and still light, the sky such a finely polished silver-blue that it looks more like a calm sea at six o'clock on a summer morning. There's one star in the west, and forty metres away in the brake the sheep carry on, making more noise than you would think sheep could.

'They'll ease off in a day or so,' Johnny says to no one directly. 'They don't know how lucky they are.'

He's right, but then it wouldn't take much to beat a bullet between the eyes and a sudden drop into a deep pit.

Johnny asks Ralph if he's fed the dogs, four of which are lying down, chins on paws. Only Rowan wanders around like an old gentleman checking all the doors are locked. The new dogs, Dusty and Dirty, lie close together.

'Yep,' says Ralph, 'and I checked their paws for grass-seeds and bindies, and they ain't got any.'

'Good.' Johnny moves one big finger around. 'We've all gotta be on the ball all the time. You've gotta look, listen and think. Keep your eyes out for anything – an open gate, bloody cars, other dogs, loose wire, snakes, fires, anything. It's what I pay you for, okay?' He seeks his answer with hard blue eyes.

'Yeah,' I say, and watch blue smoke drift off through the gums and over the horses that are roped in away from the track. Us, the horses, the sheep, the dogs, old Bett; our futures are linked like a chain.

'Beddy-byes,' I say, then yawn wide enough to stretch every one of my freckles. 'Wake me up about nine, Ralph. White tea, two sugars. I'll be in the back of old Bett.'

Johnny is unimpressed. 'Sleepin' in the ute, Lal? Ha.'

'I hate spiders,' I say. 'And if they're gonna be walking around in the dark, then I'm not gonna get in their way. See you guys later.'

'I thought I was the city slicker,' says Kate, sitting on a folded newspaper, busily filing a fingernail with the file on a red Swiss Army pocketknife.

I stop in my tracks. My fuse isn't lit, but my God it's smouldering.

'Just because I happen to hate spiders, Kate, doesn't mean I'm a wuss. And anyway, who came begging for my spare toothbrush because – ' I tap my head. ' – they'd forgotten theirs? If you were really tough, you'd go without one for two months.'

'You are a wuss, Lal,' says Ralph, ignoring the toothbrush theory. 'As far as insects and snakes and stuff goes. You're a total wuss.'

I point at the shadowy horses in their roped-off yard.

'You guys are the wusses. Hell, sitting on nags all day while I'm back here diggin' bloody firepits and toilets, chopping wood, cooking – ' I stop. Maybe Johnny doesn't get it that I'm joking, sort of? 'I'm goin' to bed. In the ute. And quit pickin' on the kid with the short hair. See you in the morning.'

I walk off. Me, soft? Geez, in Delaney Bay most people considered my whole family to be a bit on the wild side. Apart from Nadine, the hairdresser, of course. Perhaps she was adopted? I always used to tell her she was.

With a clean T-shirt on I slip into my swag, the semi-nude ham in a canvas, chilly, cotton and wool sandwich. I shine my torch on my diary, click my pen, and try to think about the day.

*8th March*

*Sawcut Creek. 10 km south of Barramah Downs. North-east NSW. Weather: Warm to hot. No clouds.*

*Our first day. Ralph and I did okay – or I hope we did. All the sheep are alive and well, anyway. Johnny watches us a lot, which is his right, but it makes me make mistakes and it makes Ralph angry. Hopefully, though, the boss'll lay off soon, and let us get on with our jobs in peace. And with a bit of luck, so will Kate. Okay, she knows what she's talking about, but it seems whatever way Ralphy and I turn, someone's giving us an earful. And Kate's accent is just about as hard to handle as Johnny's shouting. But enough of the bitching.*

*I've been thinking about the train line behind the camp and the returned soldiers who built it. I guess when they came back from the war the last* thing they wanted to do was pick and shovel work. I guess when they'd seen and been through total bloody horror, hard labour would've seemed absolutely meaningless and useless — but they took it on anyway, out in the heat and dust, month after month. Heroes I'd call them, because in the end, they did build a train line.

Sometimes you have to step right back from something to truly see that it was worthwhile. I bet those Diggers, despite everything, did try and do a good job. And so will Ralphy and I. We'll get this droving thing under control, even if it kills us. Hopefully, though, we won't have to go quite that far.

# s i x

We eat bacon and eggs and toast, drink tea, then Johnny and company move out. I wave to Ralphy as he rides by on Bruce, the horse he was on yesterday.

'Lookin' good, mate,' I say, smelling the horsy smell, hearing the creak and jangle of saddle and reins. 'Enjoy yourself.'

Ralph tosses me the last of a roll of mints trailing a wisp of silver foil. Beneath an old denim jacket we found in an op-shop he's bare chested – and looks as handsome as Ernie Dingo, but not so well fed.

'Yeah. Drive carefully. See ya.'

The drovers and the sheep wander off, leaving me with my many jobs. I check Bett's water and oil, I check the towbar and safety chain, I check the horse float and tyres, all the while experiencing a feeling of being watched. I am. By Aileen.

'I'll get to you in a sec,' I advise her. 'Stay happy.'

I pack the Dodge, check that nothing has been left lying around, then approach the big grey horse with a red rope and a secret weapon. In my pockets I have dog cubes, which Johnny tells me his horses love. I hope so. I show her a few small brown goodies.

She snuffles and whuffles enthusiastically, and brings her large horsy face in over my flat, shaky hand. I attach the red rope to her halter whilst she crunches, and watches me with calm brown eyes. Then I lead her to the horse float.

At the foot of the ramp she stops. I give her two cubes, which she takes politely from my flat paw.

'You get in,' I tell her as she chews, 'you get these.' I show her four more. 'You don't get in, I call the dog-food man.'

Aileen takes a step forward as I take a longer one back up the ramp. It seems we have the makings of a deal. Into the float I go, followed by approximately one-fifth of a horse. She pokes her nose into my shirt. Half a horse I've got now.

'Come on, Aileen! Good girl!'

Three-quarters! Four-quarters! One whole horse!

I hand over the cubes, tie off the rope, duck out the front door, nip around to the back, and lift up the ramp. Bingo! Then I sit on Bett's bonnet and give myself a five minute break to stop hyperventilating. And congratulate Johnny Hart on unlocking one of the greatest horse-training secrets of the twentieth century.

I sing as I drive, and check that Aileen's face is exactly where it should be, right behind and looking straight out of her window. It is. Good girl. I relax.

It's not that I'm totally horseophobic, if there's such a word. It's just that horses are irrational animals – and if a horse acts in an irrational way, then it stands to reason that it will be in a horse-sized way. This is one reason why guinea-pigs are such popular pets.

On the other hand, some people actually seem to enjoy riding the damn things. Perhaps I should learn, if Kate'll teach me? I could send a photo back home to Ray and Marj. They could stick me in the family album next to my brother Laurie driving his army tank, next to my sister Nadine, in her Girls 'n' Curls hairdressing salon in Melbourne. I'd be a family hero!

I think about my folks back there in Delaney Bay, tucked neatly away in their white weatherboard house . . . with the white-washed rocks out the front and the white Valiant in the drive, and Marj and Ray dressed all in white because they're maniacs for lawn bowling.

My mother wanted me to work in Delaney Bay National Bank, but having to smile at people all day would've driven me insane. And counting's never been a hobby of mine. I would've liked to go overseas – Em and I had planned to, but you know, and in the end I didn't have the money anyway.

Another good reason why I left Delaney Bay was that all the best guys also had; Nick Hahn got a job on an oil rig, Matt Holkner went to Geraldton to windsurf, Tim Morris went up to Wollongong to study. This is not to say I sat on the shelf, but the best of the rest didn't exactly thrill me. And the procession of surfers 'goin' round Austraya' in old Holden wagons were about as much use as shop dummies.

Indi Em summed it up perfectly. 'Lal,' she said once as we walked to the milk bar for litres of Coke for the surf crew, 'what are we doing hangin' around with such a bunch of turkeys?'

True. I remember that like it was yesterday: her blue thongs, my pink ones, us slapping along on the hot white footpath, plastic bottles cold against our boobs, the blue sky, the blue ocean, Crowded House on the radio, and that going-nowhere doin'-nothin' too-hot-to-think summer feeling. And then Indi got sick. A year went by. Things were hopeless. Nothing was working out like we thought it would. I couldn't face myself in the mirror.

After Indi went, I went too.

A really good thing happened today. I'm going to write it down while I remember it, and while I've got ten minutes before the sheep turn up.

9th March

*Billowbrook. 20 km from Barramah. North-east NSW.*
*Weather: hot, saw one cloud.*

*Today I drove into a tiny town called Billowbrook. Ten houses, a general store, and a single-roomed public school, all hemmed in by low brown hills. I'd stopped Bett to post a few letters we'd managed to write, and the next thing you know every kid from the entire school was lined up at the wire fence. About twenty faces, I guess, all yelling at me and Rowan the dog. Their teacher, Michael Disney, a tall skinny fella wearing a white shirt and a floral tie, came over as well.*

*Mike said that the kids and everyone else in the district knew all about the drovers with the Dodge. He reckoned that people were happy someone was making a stand, not just giving in. And that the kids were doing a class project on us. Hell, me in a class project! That's a first.*

*The kids told me about this project: what they're drawing and who's the best drawer and how hard it is to make sheep from cotton wool. And they asked questions. Like, where were we going next? How many dogs did we have? How many horses? Sheep? How come my hair was so short? Did we have a proper toilet? I bloody wish!*

Mike Disney and the kids made my day. Mike also asked me if I thought it might be a good idea to let the local television station know about us. He reckoned it might benefit the whole district to see that we're out on the road. He said, if I didn't mind, he'd call them. I said, 'Go for it!'

But later, when I told Johnny, he asked what it would prove by having a TV camera around? Nothing, I said — to us, but maybe a few other people around here might take a bit of hope from it, and that couldn't be a bad thing, could it?

Yeah I know, there I go wearing my heart on my sleeve, but in the end it paid off. Johnny didn't actually knock the idea on the head, which I suppose could mean a possible maybe. If a television crew could ever manage to find us out here, that is.

# seven

I believe I've excelled myself with tonight's fire. It blazes, sending out so much heat I feel as if my cheeks are tanning – but better than that, there's a great big, fat, ugly, hairy huntsman spider about to be swallowed by flames and sent all the way to spider hell. Johnny, with a stick, rescues it, flicking it back into the grass.

I'm appalled. 'What'd you do that for? Those things can kill you.'

The boss looks at me. 'Yeah? How?'

'By bloody fright, that's how.'

Even Kate laughs at that. It's all right for her; I'm the one who has to drag in the wood, and the buggers hide under the bark.

'Cross my heart,' I say. 'Get one of those things in your jarmies, see what happens. Dead as, mate, dead as.'

Kate and Ralph chuckle in my direction. Let 'em. Ever since I met a trapdoor spider in our laundry, it with bared fangs and me with bare feet, I've hated spiders. All spiders, except maybe daddy-long-legses.

'Speakin' of being more than a bit scared,' Johnny says, 'I'll tell you what happened once when I was shearing around Dunnington, where my grandpa was from.' He stokes the fire, sending a chorus line of sparks dancing.

A story from Johnny? This'll be interesting. Normally he uses words as sparingly as water. For the moment I put on hold all thoughts of stomping that spider, even though I know exactly where it went.

'I was just a young fella doing me first sheds,' Johnny says, 'so when I heard there was a turn down the local hall I whacked on me good clobber and limped down the hill from the property.' Johnny rubs his face, making a scratchy sound. 'Right, in I go and have a couple of dances, a bit of a yarn and a beer or two, then she's home time. So I tramped back up the hill – '

'Lal likes dancing,' Ralph says slyly. 'She practises to tapes. Jenny Morris. Don't you, Lal?'

'I do not practise,' I say, feeling my face go red. 'I just dance.'

'Let Johnny finish,' says Kate. 'Lal.'

'Yes sir,' I say, since Kate's got on a green army shirt. 'Captain.'

'Right – ' Johnny checks that Kate and I are shutting up. 'Right, it's a clear night and I'm walking along when I start gettin' a funny feeling. Like the hairs on the back of me neck are standing up. So I stop, trying to look back to where the track forks off. Nothin's there, but I wait, and I hear this sound of boots crunchin', then this bloke in old army clobber goes marchin' by on the other fork of the track.' Johnny drops a stick into the bed of glowing coals. 'So I called out, but he kept going, not lookin' sideways, and I'll tell you, I bolted like a bloody rabbit.'

Ralph moves uneasily. He and I have never really talked much about what we do or don't believe in – in the way of spirits, religion, politics, and that sort of stuff, because I think we're both scared we might totally disagree and put a hole in our friendship we couldn't fix.

'You said at the start,' I say to Johnny, 'that your grandpa was from this Dunnington joint. Was he ever in the war or anything?'

The boss nods, gives his caliper a tug to bring it around his knee a bit.

'Army. Killed in the First World War. Went away when my old man and his brother were only nippers. Never found him even. Lost in some big charge I guess. Him and a thousand others.'

A small shiver creeps up my backbone.

'And did your grandparents live anywhere near this track you were on?' Usually people who tell ghost stories aren't as hard-headed as Johnny.

'Yep, right up the hill.' Johnny expertly turns over a log and creates fire from coals.

Ralph is sitting dead still. His silence is deep and he stares intensely into the fire. I don't even feel right looking at him. Kate pulls at a loose thread until it unravels.

'There's an explanation for everything,' she says, as her button drops off. 'I think.'

'That's right,' I say, because I'm not so sure that there is. 'And the explanation is that Johnny saw a bloody ghost. Just because _you_ haven't seen one, Kate, doesn't mean they don't exist. They might.'

'I believe in 'em,' says Ralph. 'Maybe in a different kind of a way than you fellas, but I do. Who knows – ' He laughs, a gentle, thoughtful laugh. ' – what sort of things are really out there? Come on, eh?'

'Yes, Ralph,' says Kate, her voice losing half its power, 'but what I meant was your brain can suggest . . . my father says people – '

Ralph laughs again. He's cool. He sticks up for himself in the quietest possible ways – outside the boxing ring.

'We're all entitled to our opinion,' he adds. 'And Ralphy's opinion is that there are spirits out there and plenty of 'em.'

You can almost hear our brains ticking over. I let my mind go over thoughts about spirits, ghosts, and echoes . . . over thoughts about people who've gone before us, and people who are not yet born – and I come to the conclusion that all I do know is that I don't know all that much at all.

The world's a mystery to me and I like it that way. I look up into the sky, pure blackness loaded with white stars. They say it never ends. Infinity. How can that be? And that's just one thing that no one can explain. Yep, in this world, and perhaps the next, I'd say there's plenty of room for spirits and ghosts and Holy Ghosts. Plenty of room.

Luckily, Bett, loaded with my swag, is parked right in the middle of the camp – not that I'm particularly scared, of course, it's just that it's difficult to go to sleep with your eyes wide open.

I drag out my diary. From here in the back of Bett I can hear the murmur of talk as the others finish up tea and shovel dirt on the fire. I start a new page and for a while I think about Johnny's ghost story. I think about the guys who got killed in the First World War, all the thousands and thousands of them, and I also think of another person – my friend, Em. I start to write.

*Candilla Creek. 32 km south of Barramah Downs. North-east NSW.*
*Weather: dry and warm.*

*If being alive is weird – like, where do we come from and why are we here*
*– then I guess there's a big chance that when we die it's just as weird.*
*Why wouldn't a soldier from the bush always want to get back home?*
*His soul, I mean, if he'd been killed – me taking it for granted that we all*
*do have souls.*

*Look, all I'm saying is that maybe a person doesn't entirely disappear*
*when they die. I can't believe that Indi Em is not in some way around me.*
*Sometimes when I hear a certain song I can feel her presence  so incred-*
*ibly strongly. Or when I see light gliding though ripples I think of her so*
*clearly . . . I think of her because Em's soul was like that, light and*
*joyful.*

*Once Em was here right next to me – why can't she simply now have*
*gone somewhere else? Or maybe our memories of people are their spirits*
*shared between those who knew them? Maybe.*

*Today we lost our first sheep. She just sat panting and wouldn't get up.*
*I wanted to put her in the back of the ute, but Johnny said she'd had it.*
*He shot her, and that was that. Poor old girl.*

*We've been on the road now for three days. The tracks we're on wind*
*through dry brown country like powdery grey rivers with banks of tall*
*yellow grass. Dams and creeks are shrinking. Every day we look at the*
*sky for clouds. No sign of rain – or this famous TV crew, either. Maybe*
*they'll never show.*

*My arms are scratched and my fingers and wrists have got little burns all over them from the fire and the billies. But I can hack it, because the sheep are travelling well, munching along slowly . . . and who knows, tomorrow it really might rain.*

Enough. I shut my diary and turn off my torch. The camp is quiet and dark. I can hear the sheep in the brake, occasionally baaing, but they sound content, all for one and one for the other one-thousand nine-hundred and ninety-eight of them. Me too, I'm pretty happy.

# eight

After I've thrown together sand-
wiches for lunch, found one of Kate's bras left drying on
the fence, loaded Bett, and read a few pages of one of
Ralph's shonky Westerns, I leave camp. My orders are to
follow the trail of sheep manure, catch the mob about
lunchtime, and have a fire lit to boil the billies. So off I go,
me and Bett, Brucie-woose in the horse float, and Tiger the
border-collie cross in the passenger seat enjoying his ros-
tered day off.

Today's regulation ten kilometre stretch is dry. No water
for the sheep, which isn't a worry, Johnny says, if the going
is easy. All day without a drink? Not this little black duck.
I'd be delirious in fifteen minutes and seeing mirages of the
big green rock pool below the wharf at Delaney Bay, where
I had my first real kiss incidentally – which wasn't bad
either, I worked out, when I'd had a few others to compare.

I take a quick nip from my water bottle and rattle along listening to the radio, the voice riding the airwaves telling me in
dusty tones that sheep and wool prices have gone down . . .

again. In other words, if you're a sheep, start worrying. I think about our flock.

Sheep are simple critters; they go where they're pushed, mostly, they're at the mercy of everything, including drought, price falls, government policy, snakes, flies, dingoes . . . but still they walk on, growing wool, getting a fraction fatter day by day, probably dreaming of having a lamb or two. They just can't be worthless. Can they?

We devour dinner around the fire and talk about the day. I don't mention sheep or wool prices at all. Instead I drag a rock-solid round damper from the coals, knock ashes off it, and cut it up with a big black-handled knife. With the apricot jam I picked up in Yerringford, as well as a whole lot of other stuff, I'm tipping my damper'll be a taste sensation.

'Bit doughy,' says Ralph, munching. 'Me teeth are bouncin' off it.'

'Your teeth'll be bouncing off this – ' I hold up a fist. 'If you keep talking.'

Johnny eats his damper thoughtfully, but whatever thoughts he has about it he keeps to himself. He tosses the crust into the fire and puts his big enamel plate aside.

'Tomorrow,' he says, 'we'll only do six kilometres. It's breakin' the law, but if we do ten, we'll overrun the creek and the sheep'll really feel it. Just act dumb if anyone asks where we've come from. I want to leave 'em on the water for as long as possible.' Johnny looks at us levelly. 'And soon as we camp, Ralph, you wash half a dozen saddle blankets and Kate can help Lal. All right?'

We nod. We always do. I work on another shopping list. Keeping the supplies up is a pain. It's amazing how many Weetbix, bread, and apples four people can eat. As I jot down stuff I hear Kate ask Ralph if he's from New South Wales.

'Nah, Victorian side of the Murray.' He moves his feet, Cuban boot heels clacking woodenly together. 'Echuca. There's paddle steamers there and stuff. One was on a TV ad once. The *Emmy Lou*.' Ralph picks up a stick and makes a few marks in the powdery dirt. 'But my people've been there forever. Forty thousand years. In the forest. That's my place. Me relations are all round there.'

The last of the twilight hushes the sounds of the camp, the brake, and surrounding paddocks. Even the baaing and maaing of the sheep sounds as if they're wishing each other goodnight. I pretend I'm writing, but I'm actually listening to Ralph and Kate. Johnny might be too, although he has a big map spread out across his knees, a torch in his right hand.

'Must be hard for you to leave it, then?' says Kate, and her voice is quiet, too.

Ralph shrugs, runs a hand over his black fly-away hair. He glances at me.

'Yeah, but there's no jobs down there, so I had to. For a while.' The fire has all his attention now. 'I'll go back, but. Pretty soon too, I hope.' His face lifts, shadowed in the firelight. 'I don't like to leave the river too long. You know – ' He taps his chest. ' – it's in here, but that ain't the same as bein' there.'

I notice that Ralph carefully gave Kate the most obvious reason why he left Echuca – not that this is any of my business, as I've been so loudly told.

Kate nods, no doubt thinking that the differences between her and Ralph Kiddle are as wide as old man Murray River himself – and I guess they are, and they aren't. Spanning the gap between them, between all of us, is a fine web of things we all have in common: hope for the future, like wanting to get somewhere, like being good at something, like not wanting to sink like a stone and get stuck in the mud.

'Well, if along the Murray's your place,' Kate says, 'you're lucky. It's beautiful. I tried to write a poem about the sound of a river once. It didn't work out.'

Ralph rearranges his hat, giving himself time to consider what he's been told.

'Yeah, I am lucky,' he says finally. 'Some people don't belong anywhere. I always belong near the river. It'll do me, when I get back there. Even if it is stinkin' hot in summer.'

And where does little old Lal-pal belong? In some dreary little town? Wandering around the CES boards? Pulling beers in a pub with a flickering TV and an aching back for company? Bludging on the beach because I've got nothing else to do? Geez, I hope not. I slide a careful look at Kate and try to suss out what she's thinking. Her curved face gives away as little as a cover girl's. Whether she knows it or not, she's got a safety net below her that'll never let her down. She'll never not have a job, or money, or a place to live. All she has to do is play it safe and her family'll always have what it takes to make sure she's okay. Whereas the safety nets that hang below Ralphy and me are not quite so reliable. We're the ones who should be playing it safe, but we're not.

Kate gets up, smacking dust from her jeans, silver fly buttons showing. I can imagine her at uni parties, probably near a Sydney beach, all the people nice looking and shower-fresh – no dirty aggro dudes turning up in hotted-up yellow station wagons with AC/DC blasting. Still, if guys like that did turn up I doubt it'd faze Kate out. She'd just call the police. No, she wouldn't – she could handle it. She's tough enough, in a career girl kind of a way.

Kate pulls up a maroon-and-white Sea Eagles football sock. She even plays touch footy. She showed me a scar.

'Put you on a horse tomorrow, Lal. Aileen's perfect for you.'

She is? That big grey lump? God, we hardly even speak to each other.


A white utility is parked in the shade of a big gum. A bloke wearing dark glasses, khaki shorts, khaki shirt and grey hat is leaning arms-crossed against it. He moves away from the ute as soon as he sees Bett. I brake and stop. It's a council vehicle, with a coat of arms and Shire of Yerringford painted in red on the door. The guy saunters around to my window, which is Rowan's chance to go absolutely haywire. I tell him to shut up and siddown in the bloody back. He does, unbelievably.

'Gidday,' I say, 'bit warm.' I can't see a thing behind the sunglasses. Perhaps he's got no eyes?

'Yeah.' The council guy bats at flies. 'It is. You with the drovers?'

'Yeah,' I say, answering with as little friendliness as he's asking.

'I'm the shire ranger,' he adds, not looking at me but past me, inspecting the gear piled high in the back of Bett. 'Goin' all right, is it?'

'Fine,' I say, aware of the sweat on my forehead now that I've stopped, and of my hot cheeks.

Dark glasses are brought back in my direction. He's got a crooked nose, which doesn't surprise me. Someone's probably objected to his manner, with a right hook.

'Know about the ten kilometre a day rule, do you?' he asks.

'Yeah,' I say. 'We always do 'em.' So far we have, anyway.

His hat brim drops, and wouldn't you know it? It's a Greg Norman 'great white shark' hat – but somehow I can't see this bloke on a golf course. I doubt he'd be able to scrape up three friends.

'You better be doing 'em,' he says heavily, 'because it's easily checked. Farmers round here aren't real keen on drovers. Never have been for that matter. Takin' their feed and water, leaving busted bottles and smoulderin' fires.'

That's not what Mike Disney said, but I keep that to myself. The Great White Shire Shark takes a step back.

'Don't you go breakin' no fences or laws. I'll see you.'

Not if I see you first, I think to myself, and drive off, looking in my mirror, seeing him writing something down in a small black book.

# nine

Another day, another morning without a shower. I fill a bucket from a jerrycan, then armed with my health bag, as it was known at Delaney Bay Primary, I set off for my open-air bathroom. I even scramble through a barbed-wire fence – after all, if someone sees young Lal in the nude, they might indeed decide there are fairies at the bottom of the garden, and stick me in a sideshow.

And don't think I haven't seen *The Elephant Man* movie, because I have.

I strip off, feet crackling crinkle-cut leaves and bone-dry sticks. The sun's just up, balancing on a treetop, a few fleecy clouds separating it from the cool, blank sky. There's a farmhouse too, surrounded by three generations of sheds. All quiet up there, though.

I rub my wet self all over with cold soap until each and every goosebump has been covered, then I rinse, watching freckles reappear. As soon as I get to work with my towel I decide it's definitely worth the shivers; I always feel 99 per cent better when I smell reasonable, and to step into clean undies and socks is the drover's version of power dressing for the office. Bad luck about the grubby jeans and shirt, but. Buttoned and buckled up I walk back through damp grass, and see that Ralph has the fire going and billies on. What a guy!

'Good job,' I say, as I dump my bucket. 'So what d'you reckon about all that on this fine day?' I wave a hand around.

Ralph kneels, poking sticks under the billies to get them firing. He blows on them to get a few stubborn flames happening, then squats stockman-style.

'Johnny's treatin' me like a kid, fair dinkum.' He sniffs, a hard fast effective boxer's sniff that's as aggressive as a grunt. 'He's always watchin' me and telling me stuff I already know.' He spits over clasped hands, spit sizzling on burning sticks. 'Still, yeah, you know, it's okay. Ralph Kiddle can handle it.'

I flick one of his dusty kneecaps.

'Course you can, mate.' I squat down too, feeling like a cowboy. 'Look, yesterday he asked me if I knew what sort of petrol to put in the bloody truck.' This is true. 'So I said yeah, ultra bloody unleaded.'

Ralph smiles slowly, against his will. I guess this is the same kind of question he's been getting from the boss; crap that we do know, but if by some chance we don't, then it could cause a major stuff-up. Johnny's just being extra careful. Still, it gets to you, being treated like a dummy. I lift off a boiling billy with a stick and pour water onto teabags.

'Just stick to your guns, eh?' I say, putting the billy back. 'He'll figure it out sooner or later, or maybe he'll lighten up when we get some rain.' I shovel sugar into our cups, watching it dissolve like the lines of frustration in Ralphy's face.

'Yeah, I guess.' Ralph absorbs his anger, his hands loosening and his fingers linking – and I can see why he is angry – because it's always us, the guys down the bottom of the work

71

ladder who have to cop whatever's being handed out. But that's the way it is, and probably always has been.

Now, for some reason, I ask Ralph straight out why he left Echuca so suddenly. The question catches us both off guard.

His hands break apart and he takes a fast look around the camp. I also look, but Johnny and Kate are miles away with the horses, feeding them oats from a green plastic bin.

'Okay, Lal,' Ralph says warily and wearily. 'Okay. All right, I'll tell you. I don't really wanna, but I will. It's only gonna cause trouble. You wanna hear it, you sure?'

Of course I'm sure!

'Maybe I can help,' I say, and I squat stockman-style too. 'I'm your mate aren't I, remember?'

'Okay.' Ralph's hands flutter once. 'Okay, there was these two blokes down home, white fellas, real losers, and they were draggin' Murray cod and yellowbelly out of the river illegal. Like with drum nets and even dynamite someone said.' Ralph's hands glide now. 'The fish and that river are pretty special to us so – anyway – ' He stops. I can hear the sizzle of boiling water. 'That kind of stuff makes me really angry.'

'Yeah,' I say, 'I understand that. And – ?'

'Well, one night I was fishing by myself – ' Ralph checks again that Johnny or Kate aren't coming across from the horses. 'And I run into one of these bastards and we had a blue.'

Ralph stands, folds his arms, looks down at the seething water.

'Yeah, and I give him a decent hiding. He had miles of bloody lines with him, the bloody thief. Then his mate turned up with a bloody rifle, so I took off into the bush – ' Ralph looks at me, then shakes his head. 'Then the fella I belted turned up a week later down Gunbower Weir, rolled up in his own lines, dead as a doornail.'

'Dead?' I say stupidly, and I also get up. 'Dead?'

Ralph grabs my arm. His pupils are like black bullets.

'Didn't have nothin' to do with me, Lal. I only give him a few whacks and told him to keep off the river. I swear.'

Tea slops over the edge of my mug, scalding my finger. Someone dead. God. You can't get much more serious than that.

'So why'd you leave town then?' I ask, and hold my fingers against the coolness of my jeans. 'You shouldn't have split, mate, if you had nothin' to do with it. It would've been cleared up and – '

Ralph looks at me as if I'm slow. I guess I am sometimes.

'Because that bloke who saw me might've seen me again, and dobbed me in to the coppers. He could've said I chucked his mate in the bloody river, who knows? And maybe the coppers'll believe the whitefella before the blackfella. It can happen, Lal. It has before.' Ralph stares hard at me, as if I don't believe him, but I do. 'I didn't chuck him in, Lal. On my mother's grave I didn't. D'you believe me?'

The story's replaying in my head. Night by a big wide river. A fight. Someone turning up with a gun. Deep water. High banks. I . . . do believe him.

'You're a fighter, mate,' I say, 'but you're no killer.' I ask him if he told anyone else about the fight.

He shakes his head. 'Nobody. No one knew except the bloke's mate. So I didn't want to bump into him again, did I? Just told me dad I was leavin' to go to me cousin's place up Queensland to look for work.'

I've got a hundred questions, but they'll all have to wait, because Kate's coming over, bashing at her hair with a brush. My brush actually – not that I need it much these days. She lost hers who knows where. Or how.

'Putting on the L-plates this afternoon, Lal,' she says. 'Remember? The horsey?'

Damn. I'd forgotten all about my famous riding lesson. Ralph's story has knocked me for six. I kneel and start to flick yellow blobs of margarine into the two big silver frypans.

'Can't wait,' I lie, and go back to cracking heads, er, I mean eggs.

# t e n

Most days – well, six or seven times in the two weeks since leaving Barramah Downs, people stop me for a yak session. It seems we're the first drovers to use these back roads for twenty years, which has turned us into something of a travelling talk show.

This morning an old lady in a bottle-green cardigan and black gumboots flags me down. I stop Bett next to an open front gate so buckled it'll never be shut.

'I thought you was the postman,' she says sternly, gripping a heavyweight walking stick with a gnarled, knuckly hand. 'But you're with them drovers, aren't you?'

I say I am, feeling as if I'm being accused of something.

A yellow dog comes belting down the drive, barking without taking a breath. It's told to shut up. It does, but growls and prowls, looking half-ready to spring at me or Dusty-dog, a kelpie, who's busily growling back. I decide I don't like this place or this person all that much.

'You're wasting your time with them sheep,' the old lady tells me. 'No money in 'em these days. They're worthless.' She stands in the middle of her driveway, holding onto a handker-chief and a stick, a bent-over figure in a ragged sun-smashed landscape.

I don't get angry. I don't even think she particularly means what she's saying. I think she's simply finished with anything at all hopeful. By the look of the place, branches fallen over fences, the shearing shed showing its rafters like sagging bones, there hasn't been too much to be hopeful about around here for years.

'Things can change,' I say, not loudly. 'It'll rain. Prices'll go up. People'll realise wool's better than man-made. Our boss reckons it ain't time to give up yet.'

The old lady draws herself back into her cardigan as if it was cold. I feel guilty about my warm bare arms. I try to imag-ine the lines and sunspots leaving her old face, the wrinkles softening away, her hair colouring back to gold, until she's young, a girl, round-wristed and straight-backed. She would've been hopeful then.

'How long have you lived here?' I ask suddenly.

She lifts her stick in the direction of a house hidden by dark trees bowed by winds that occasionally ease off, but always come back.

'Too bloody long. Sixty-one years. In there.' She grips her stick fiercely, then rests on it, her other hand rearranging her cardigan. 'I got stuck with it, and I'm still stuck with it.' She turns, about to make her way back up the drive. 'You be care-ful,' she says, and slowly walks off, back to her kitchen, I guess. And teapot and TV and dog.

'You too,' I call out.

I drive off, but it takes more than a few turns of the road before I feel like singing with the radio again.

After I've got the camp into the order I hope Commandant
Johnny will approve of, I spend five minutes chucking stones
at a can on a stump, just for the hell of it. Then I drag out my
diary. I think about the old lady I talked to today. Geez, life
can trap you so tight you can struggle for fifty years and never
get away. Then you just have to give up. I click my pen and
try to get some stuff down that's not too stupid.

*20th March, maybe 21st*

*Piah Creek, North-east NSW.*
*Weather: warm.*

*What might that old lady have hoped for when she was younger? When
luck and time hadn't run out on her? What did she dream of? Something
simple, like two good years for the farm in a row, or for one of the kids to
do really well — but whatever it was it didn't happen, or the power of it
didn't last the years. Facts cut through dreams like a knife through
Christmas wrapping paper. Ask Ralph about his title fight, or Johnny or
Dell about getting their property up and running.*

*Look, we can't all be high-fliers, I know that — but no one wants to spend
their life doing work they hate. And no one wants to spend their days
waiting for the empty-handed postman in Missed Chance, that dead-end
place where life ticks by like an old clock in a dark room. I sure as hell
don't. I'm on the lookout for a way out, because if you don't look, you'll
never find.*

I shut my diary, depressed, and as I stash it I think about
Ralph's fight back in Echuca. I believe his story, but he could
be in strife if certain other people don't. Maybe this other guy
just fell in the river anyway? The whole thing's probably

finished with and forgotten. Probably. Certainly. I make up my mind not to mention it again. Let sleeping dogs lie.

Kate appears, leading Aileen, who clomps along behind, ears twitching.

'Come here, Lal.'

For God's sake, what does she want now? Oh no, the bloody horse.

'Nah, sorry, I've got all this – '

'Come on, Lal, don't be so gutless.'

Gutless? I get up. Gutless? Careful.

I walk over and find myself face to face with Aileen. She gazes at me, I don't look at her. Kate shakes a stirrup, then pats the bump at the front of the saddle.

'Hand up here, boot in there. I'll hold her while you get on.'

I'm not convinced. Surely there should be a few hours of theory first?

'Get on, Lal. Hurry up.'

'Yes, boss.' I go to get on. Obviously from my instructor's negative body language I have already committed a serious boo-boo.

'This side, Lal. Dork.'

'Yes, boss. Sorry, boss.' I walk around the horse. She's large. With a huge amount of effort I actually do get on. Streuth, it's high up here. I can see right through the trees to where the sheep are settled in the brake. Without warning Aileen drags the reins out of my hands. And now she's munching grass, tearing off mouthfuls.

Kate recaptures the reins and shows me how to hold them. She tells me to sit up straight, keep my heels down, and to relax. Then with one small grunt she springs up on Massy and I slowly follow them out of the camp, sort of plonking along on top, with two sweaty paws and a worried mind.

Up the old track we wander, me not even game enough to swish at the flies.

'This is as fast as I'll ever go,' I tell Kate's hat and ponytail. 'Galloping and that sort of thing is for loonies.'

Kate laughs at me, which makes me angry, but not angry enough to lose concentration. Otherwise I might fall off. We go on, clip-clopping through a late afternoon of stretching shadows and flocks of gabbling galahs settling in favoured trees. It's not unpleasant. In fact I'm in danger of quite liking it, even though swaying has never been one of my greatest skills. The heat of the afternoon has gone and the hills around us look like great big yellow pears in a fruit bowl.

Around a corner, beating up brown dust, comes a white utility. It stops in front of the horses. It's the ranger from Yerringford Shire, still wearing the dark glasses and shark hat. He gets out and waits for us to walk up to him. I pray Aileen won't do anything stupid, like run away. She stops when Massy stops, and chews on her bit with a hard grating sound.

'Got a message for your boss,' says the man with no eyes. And a very small chin, I notice.

'Oh yeah,' I say, whilst Kate says nothing.

The shire ranger flicks open his white pad and studies it for a moment.

'On the 21st of March drovers passing through Yerringford Shire did not complete the required ten kilometres of travel.' He looks up at us. 'I won't go into details, but I could make it bloody hard for you. I could but I won't, because you'll be out of my shire by tomorrow, or you'd better be. Ya understand?'

His shire? His? I nod but say nothing. The horses move

their feet and cicadas churn out a river of noise. The ranger walks back to his utility and stops at the door.

'This part of the country ain't as friendly as you think. It's hard enough for the locals to survive, let alone with you comin' through and taking what's not yours to take. Make sure your boss gets the message. Keep movin'.'

He gets into the vehicle, swings a U-turn, and drives past us, tyres spitting stones and lifting dust. Aileen rocks like a big ship, moves half a metre sideways, but doesn't do anything impolite. I'm beginning to like her.

Kate watches the car go. 'In a perfect world,' she says, 'you'd be allowed to punch someone like that. Probably wears leopard print underpants, too. Nylon.'

I laugh. She's got it in one. I pull gently on the left-hand rein and Aileen turns awkwardly but apparently happily.

'We'd better go tell Johnny, I guess,' I say, trying not to show how pleased I am that my first command to a horse has been promptly obeyed. 'Pass on the good news.'

# eleven

Tonight's fire blazes, bright flames creating a gang of shadows that lurk in the trees. The flock is quiet and so are the dogs, but in the distance I hear the occasional crack and boom of someone shooting, spotlighting.

Johnny, as he repairs his caliper with thick green cord, asks Ralph how he got started in the boxing business.

'You knock a few kids out at school, then make a living out of it?'

'Nah,' says Ralph. 'Never had many fights at school.' He smears Vegemite on a toasted crust. 'This old local bloke got me started. He grabbed me an' me mate Dezzy because we were knockin' off his beer bottles to sell, but instead of giving us a hidin' he let us have a go on this punchin' bag he had set up.' Ralph holds up his hands, the crust balanced on his knee. 'He gave us the basics and let us hammer away. Told us how a good boxer's gotta be fit and full of guts, so I reckoned – ' Ralph lets us have a dry smile. ' – I'd have a go.' He stops, looking towards the brake where the sheep are settled.

We look too, like we do every couple of minutes without even realising, but the sheep are quiet. Ralph undoes a shirt button, exposing a triangle of smooth brown skin.

'Anyway, Lyle trained me up for me first amateur fights and I used to help him cart wood. He was a real good bloke. Knew about all the Aboriginal fighters, too. Knew where they come from and who they fought and what happened to 'em.' Ralph shrugs. 'I had a few pro fights, but I always trained with Lyle. Then I lost a couple –' Ralph glances at me across the top of the fire. 'So in the end I had to take off from town to find work. Ended up in Barley's tent. Had some good times though, didn't we, Lal?'

We did.

'We sure did,' I say. 'It was a bit of a classic, that joint.'

It was. Under the faded canvas of Danny Barley's stinking old green tent we lived whole lifetimes in three-minute rounds. The place had the same creepy, deadly fascination as a pit of snakes. There was Danny Barley prowling around, snake charmer and keeper all rolled into one, challenging the locals to get up and have a go. And they always did.

And there were our fighters, resting out the back in ragged dressing gowns – or out the front fighting, sweating, jabbing, hooking, circling, waiting to strike. Or getting struck, because on a bad night someone would get pounded. And on the tent walls a painted parade of world champs always danced and jabbed as the canvas breathed in and out like the living green lung of some prehistoric swamp monster.

I hated the tent and I loved it. It was seedy all right – a quick trip back to the bad old days, but sometimes it was hilarious and silly. It was unforgettable, that's what it was. Barley's boxing tent. Someone should make a movie. Or at least tell the story.

Maybe that's why I keep my diary, to make sure there's a record, however bad, of what did happen.

'Ralph can sure box,' I tell Johnny and Kate. 'For every fight he lost he won ninety-nine.'

'Copped a few hidings, but,' Ralph adds evenly. 'There's always some bloke out there who can take you apart. You don't want to reckon anyone's too easy.' He lifts his eyebrows.

Through the trees, maybe a kilometre away, I see a sliver of white light roaming and roving the paddocks. Johnny's also noted the light, but it's not the light he talks about.

'My old man,' says the boss drover, 'rest in peace, reckoned Lionel Rose was the best boxer he'd ever seen. Said he had the works. Fitness, defence, speed, guts, the lot.' Johnny holds up a hand that looks like something you'd buy from a hardware shop. 'He woulda made a beautiful shearer. You interested in shearing at all, Ralph?'

'Yeah,' says Ralph carefully, 'I said to Lal when we was watching you at the show that I wouldn't mind havin' a go at it.'

'I'll keep that in mind,' says Johnny.

For fifteen minutes we've listened uneasily to the crack of rifles and the boom of shotguns, and watched as two dead-straight beams of white light carve and cut across dry grass and scaly-barked trees. Johnny tells Ralph to stoke up the fire.

'Let 'em know we're here. And – ' The boss stands, flexing rather than stretching. 'If these clowns do come past, everyone does exactly what I say and when I bloody say it, all right? Everyone.'

We nod, the sick feeling in my stomach thickening as three fast rifle shots hammer holes in the blackness. A car engine revs, I hear shouting.

'Right, that's it,' says Johnny. 'They're comin'.'

We get up, waiting to be told what to do. A spotlight slides down a hill then leaps up into the treetops. Johnny gives orders.

'Kate, run an extra rope around the horses. Ralph, catch the dogs and tie 'em. Lal, start the ute and put the lights on. And everyone, keep outta the way and keep your eye on the sheep. If they get out on the road – just make sure they don't.'

We split up.

'Lal, keep real low in the ute, all right? Under the bloody dashboard.'

Absolutely.

'Everybody, heads down!' Johnny picks up the axe and another torch and heads out to the road.

I slide into the ute, my stomach doing a flip as a shotgun booms. Ralph runs past with a handful of chains and a pack of struggling dogs.

Bett starts first hit, I turn on the headlights, and toe them on to full beam. Eighty metres up the track I see the glint and gleam of chrome and paint. Headlights cut and sway, the bush seems to bounce back and forward. Someone yells over a honking horn.

'Eh! What's the big bloody idea!' The voice, rough as hurled gravel, is aimed at us from over an elbow out of the window of a white F-100 utility. 'Turn your flamin' lights off, ya dickheads!'

A spotlight invades the camp, scooting over the fire, chairs, and swags, to seize on Bett. I duck, whacking my head on the steering wheel as whiteness explodes into the cab. Shit that's bright. Hell my head hurts.

'No!' Johnny yells. 'You get your frigging lights off us! We got two thousand bloody sheep here! Piss off with those guns!'

In loyalty to our boss I sit up. There are two utilities out on the track now, a battered old bronze Valiant stopped a few metres behind the Ford. There are also plenty of guys, guns, and spotlights. Bull-bars glint, dust drifts over the ground, engines tick over fast and loud.

'Get off the track, yer bloody drongo! We're comin' through!' There's laughter and the sound of a half-full can smacking into a tree.

In the flaring white light Johnny is illuminated like the statue of a bushman on a stage, complete with an axe. Everything looks grey-blue or white, all outlines stark, all noises loud and harsh. Our dogs are going berserk. I can hear the sheep and they don't sound happy at all. The night's packed tight with noise.

'Get outta the way, Limpy! Shift yer arse!' More laughter, another flying can.

The white Ford turns on driving lights. Johnny moves to the edge of the track, standing head down against the white glare, elbow out as he grips the axe. I can see the outline of two or three guys in the back of the Ford ute, guns poking upwards. In the Valiant there's another two. Guns, I keep thinking. Guns.

Johnny's head lifts. 'Yeah, well go bloody past then. Just kill the bloody lights and watch those bloody guns!' He stands where the grass meets the track, our territory.

The sheep are baaing and maaing and our dogs bark non-stop, dragging Ralphy around as he tries to hold them back beyond the fire. From the old Valiant a heavy white dog is dropped over the side. A bull-terrier cross, by the look of the boxy head on it. A studded collar, like a band of steel, is tight around its neck.

'Sic 'em, Freddy!' The dog runs a few steps, then stops, confused. 'Go on, yer bloody mongrel! Go!' The dog comes into the camp, snout aimed, mouth open, looking for something to fight.

The scared feeling in my stomach balloons, but it's now hard-edged with a kind of tribal anger. Stuff this other mob! I scramble out of Bett and run towards Ralph to help him with the sheepdogs. The shooter's mutt keeps on coming, not running but just about to, its eyes glowing red in the lights. A spotlight locks on Ralph, freezing him in white light.

'Get the boonger, Freddy! And his bloody mongrels!'

'Steady on, Gaz,' says a voice from the cabin of the big white Ford. 'I gotta bit of blackfella in me too, remember.'

The white dog starts to run at our dogs. I take three quick steps and as it gallops past I kick it in the ribs as hard as I can. Thud. Goal! Mark that one down in your footy record. It turns, snarling, looking absolutely wicked. I jump back, fear clawing.

'Garn!' I shout, not very convincingly. 'Piss off!' It doesn't, it takes two tiny steps then sets itself to – Ralph lets our dogs go, they charge, and Kiddle's charging after them.

Instantly there's a whirlpool of snarling, biting bodies, with Ralph right in the middle. He plunges a hand down, grabs the shooters' dog by the collar, hefts it, and belts it hard with the heel of his hand. Then he flings it away and somehow manages to get hold of all but one of the sheepdogs. The white mongrel backs away, dazed and spotted with blood, Dusty-dog seeing it off with a volley of barks and growls.

'Jesus – ' A hard voice arrows at me from the Valiant ute. 'Check the short-haired sheila. Ug-lee as!'

They'll have to do better than that to get me going. I've heard worse from ten-year-old kids. And I could give far worse back, but I keep quiet. Even though I've got hold of a decent stick I could score a direct hit with from here. But I don't hurl it, because there's one thing I do know about guys for sure;

you dint their car, they go mental. I don't even tell them to drop dead. Instead I catch Dusty, and a heap more names. It's pathetic.

'Hey, slag! You get nothin' outta ten!'

'Come 'ere, moll! You'll do.'

Laughter. Loud voices in the dark. I hope they all die in a car accident. Tonight hopefully. And I think to myself that the old 'sticks and stones' saying is crap. Names can hurt all right, but right now I'm letting them simply sail right on over my head. They keep coming though, a barrage from brains filled with nothing.

'And you, you useless black bastard. Piss off!'

'And take white trash with yer!'

I look at Ralph and I'm scared of what I see. Even in the dark I can tell his eyes are as hard and cold as two old iron spikes.

'Ignore 'em, Ralphy!' I yell over the noise and rubbish and crap. 'They're morons, mate. They're nothin' but – ' I move towards him, reaching for his arm, but I miss by a centimetre.

Ralph drops the dog chains, spins away from me and runs, straight into a storm of dust, white light, hurled cans, and insults.

'Yeah, come on, ya stupid drongo!'

'Why doncha bring ya sheila with ya?'

'Ralph!' I yell, scrabbling for the dog chains. 'Ralphy! Don't!'

Johnny turns, sees Ralph as he's just about to pass him, lunges and misses, thrown off balance by his calipered leg. Ralph veers past the big white Ford and with one jump leaps over the bullbar and onto the bonnet – crunch! – of the bronze Valiant. His second step takes him onto its roof, the next he disappears into the back of it, fists flying. I pick up my stick and run, following Johnny who's dropped the axe and is moving with pace I didn't know he had.

The doors of the Ford fly open, guys jumping out of the cabin and down from the back like rats from a burning ship. One turns, waiting for me, ready to grab or hit.

'Ya ugly little – '

I swing the stick, and catch the back of a fist. It makes a sound like a cricket bat hitting a hard ball. The bloke staggers back swearing. I go past – the next thing I know I'm rolling off the track into the scrub, sticks spiking me, leaves rasping me, dust choking up my nose and in my eyes. Someone's belted me or shirt-fronted me or something. I get up, but only just. I stand, lean against a friendly tree, and watch dizzily.

Ralph is hitting and being hit. Hands and arms are trying to hold him, but he's too fast and wild. His fists are flying and so's Johnny. He pounces, grabs one bloke by the waist and wrenches him off the ute and throws him face down into the dirt. He grabs the next bloke who instantly clocks him with an elbow. Whack! Johnny staggers back, regains his balance, then is knocked flat as Ralph punches a guy in a black T-shirt right out of the utility and directly on top of him. Now Ralph's alone up there, as if this is a game of no-holds-barred king of the castle. Two shadows come at him from behind.

'Behind you, Ralph!' I shout, but they grab him and try to tear him off the tray.

He thrashes, throwing a flurry of quick short punches, but they've got him, and they let him have it on the way down with their free hands. I run, following Johnny who's roaring like a bull.

'That's enough! Enough! Cut it out! Enough! Cut it out! Now!'

And for some reason they do. They sling Ralph out onto the road and straighten up, heaving for breath, but ready for more. Guys are milling about, two with guns, and the bloody white dog's licking my hand as if he's mine. I decide not to kick it again in case it bites my leg off.

A big dark bare-bellied guy with a black beard and a shotgun is yelling what Johnny's yelling.

'Yeah, back off, everyone! That's it. All over. No more. Back off, Danny. You too, Jeff. Garn. That's it. All over. Come on, calm down. Fun's over.'

The two sides sort themselves out, Johnny getting to Ralph, pulling him back down the road and calling out to me.

'Get here, Lal. Don't stuff around. Move!'

I start for the camp but I don't go down the road, no fear. I'm not going anywhere near the guy I hit with the stick. Through the trees I sneak, watching the other blokes getting back into the utes as motors are gunned. Someone fires a shotgun, orange flame stabbing up into blackness.

'Yeeehaaaa!'

My stomach contracts like a burst bubble.

'Whoohaaa!' More gunshots, booming and sudden, orange spikes of flame stabbing up in the smoky blackness. 'Yaaagh! Haagh!'

I make it into the camp, grab the dogs, and drag them behind Bett. Ralph and Johnny walk in from the track, the two of them looking as if they've been hit and run over by stampeding cattle. A voice blasts out of the cabin of the big white ute.

'See you, cobbers! Nice to meetcha!'

Yeah, sure. I laugh, with my mouth shut, and watch the two utilities backing up, floating on clouds of dust. The Valiant turns, and right there in the driver's seat I see a face I remember real well: the guy from Yerringford Shire Council. The bloody ranger! He's sitting there with a stupid, evil smile on his face and now he gives me a friendly little wave. What a low life! I bet it was him who directed his wood duck mates down here – I bend, grab the tomato sauce bottle by the neck, take it back, take aim . . . then lower it.

What's the use? People like that are simply born ugly inside and out and stay that way forever. Forget it. It'd be just a waste of good tomato sauce. A musical car horn honks, da-dah, dah-dah dah-da da-duh! A slab of wood comes bouncing down the track. I hear Kate shouting, her voice coming out of the darkness.

'Quick! The brake! Quick! It's going over!'

We run towards the bulging brake, and as we run I feel sick because I know that Ralph and I've failed. We've stuck up for each other, but we didn't do our bloody jobs. We've failed like we've never failed before.

I throw myself at the brake. Ralph and I are losers. We're stupid, we're hopeless, we're – no wonder we're gettin' nowhere. God, we're going bloody backwards.

Sheep rush this way then that like swilling water. The noise is loud and I can feel the heat of the mob coming back at me, a humid, smelly fog. I hold onto the stake with all my might, hoping, willing the sheep to try and run right over me so I can be a hero – because I know that even though Ralphy and I might've won the fight, as far as Johnny's concerned, we lost the battle by a country mile.

We keep the sheep in the brake. They mill and they baa, they strain at the stakes and the netting, but they stay where they are. I thank my lucky stars. For half an hour we work at shoring everything up, Johnny wielding the hammer, talking to us only when he has an order to give. Ralph and I don't say a word to each other or anyone else. If it's possible to make up for our mistakes we're already trying to do it. Eventually we go back to the fire and the billy is boiled.

'Okay,' says Johnny finally, taking a mug of tea from Kate. 'Okay. The only thing I'm gonna say is from now on if I give someone a job they better bloody do it no matter what. I don't care, Ralph and Lal – ' He looks at us until I feel like crying. ' – what anyone says to you, because it's bullshit and doesn't matter. Your job is what matters. The sheep.' Johnny points at us with the mug, which looks like a big green boxing glove on the end of his hand. 'Tonight was your fault. You made it ten times worse than it had to be. Tonight was a chance for you to prove you're real drovers, but you both stuffed up. And don't think I won't sack you out here because I bloody-well will.'

Silence, harder to bear than words. I can feel Johnny's anger and accusations buzzing around me like a swarm of wasps.

'Sorry,' says Ralph, his voice husky and broken. 'We did the wrong thing. We should've stuck with the sheep. I know it. Sorry.'

'Me, too,' I say. 'Sorry.'

The boss leans back in his canvas chair just as he does every night, but he looks neither relaxed or calm. Kate says nothing, looking down at her hands clasped between her knees. Ralph and I don't look at each other. The boss sips tea, then puts his mug down in the dust.

'Okay, tomorrow's another day. Just remember what I said about your jobs. And remember what you said about 'em as well, that you could do 'em.' He leans away from us and clears his nose into the dust. Spots of blood dot his face. He nods at Ralph and I. 'Jesus, don't just sit there, you two. Go and get the bloody first-aid box and fix yerselves up. You look rough as guts.'

Ralph and I obediently stand up and walk away from the fire. I feel as if I've been court-martialled.

*

The camp is empty, the sheep gone, the truck packed, Bruce the horse is tied by the float. I sit near the fire, open my diary, the sun bouncing off the page so brightly I have to get up and move into the shade. It's the 30th of March. I write that down.

*30th March*

*10 km from Piah Creek. North-east NSW.*
*Weather: hot, a few clouds, no wind.*

*Well, it's been an action-packed twenty-four hours and Ralphy and I have proved ourselves to be a couple of untrustworthy hooligans.*

*Johnny was right about us wasting a big chance to show that we're reliable. It's more than the fact that he's our boss and we're paid to look after his sheep. Droving's a job where your whole character's involved. You are the job. You don't just give two hundred bucks a week worth of droving, then knock off. You have to mould yourself around the work, take crap from morons if need be, get heatstroke if need be, break the law if need be, or a leg — but look after the bloody sheep.*

*Okay, Ralphy and I understand that now. We thought we did before, but we didn't. I could make excuses for us, but I won't. We'll just have to try harder. It's all we can do.*

# twelve

The sun crosses the sky as slow-moving as the hands of a factory wall clock. Each day is another dot on the big blue calendar, marked by pink sunrises and orange sunsets. Over two hundred kilometres the sheep have walked, living on yellow bristly grass and green or brown water. When is it going to rain? I don't know, but what I do know is that it must rain soon because if it doesn't, we'll run out of water, and then we'll run out of time. Without water we have to stop, and when we stop, the rifles'll come out. And that'll be that.

I look up at the sky. There are clouds, clouds as white and dry and useless as scrunched-up old tissues. Bett and I drive on, through a landscape that waits silently and pants, heat shimmer the only thing that softens the outlines at all.

Today there's no town, no supermarket for me to visit and enjoy. I've passed farmhouses, waved to a lady hanging out sheets, waved to two young guys in big hats hanging a gate, and a girl riding a spotty brown horse, but that's about the extent of my social interaction. And now I'm about to walk back to meet the sheep, for something to do.

I'm ambling along beside Ralphy and Charlie-horse the chestnut. A creek, more of a marsh, has managed to smudge a line of green grass through a decent-looking paddock, but the fence beside us is standing about as solidly as a one-legged high jumper with an uphill start. Ralph sends Tiger out to patrol the wire. I pluck at a rusty strand of number eight gauge.

'Reckon old Farmer Brown's been a bit slack,' I say. 'This whole thing's about to lie down and die.' Fence posts, just managing to do their job, stand like decaying teeth. I reckon, even off a short run-up, I could kick them over.

Ralph stands in his stirrups to check on Tiger's progress.

'Only gotta last two more minutes and we'll – geez, it's bloody gone!'

Kate, ahead and out on the left of the mob, yells as she wheels Massy towards the collapsed fence.

'Go onnn, sheep! Go! Get! Johnny! Quick! Over here!'

I start running, thinking Kate'll block the hole before me. She doesn't. She moves on up the road – the wrong way, I reckon, but it's too late to worry about that now. Johnny I can't see, but I can sure hear him. His voice seems to be coming from the right-hand side of the mob, where I saw him tooling along earlier on Bruce.

'Get in that bloody hole, Kate!' he shouts, stranded in a sea of shifting sheep. 'Kate! Kate, Jesus – Lal! You bloody go! Get goin'!'

I go, and the sheep go too. And left and right, centre, and sideways. Ahead a stream of woolly runaways pour into the paddock over flattened wire, two posts lying down like skittled pedestrians.

Where the snapped posts are I make my stand. I'm shouting like a madwoman confronting a foyer-full of bargain hunters charging for the escalators. Sheep surround me, baaing pitifully, showing off furry tongues and grass-stained teeth. I kick, whack, and push until the Kamikaze avalanche of chump chops begins to reverse. Dust rises, dogs bark, everyone is shouting but I am by far the loudest.

'Garn! Gerrout! Skat! Shoo!'

Suddenly, sheep-like, mass escape turns into mass obedience. Kate rides past to help me out. With one all-out effort I manage to lift the fallen fence and keep it propped. Tiger and Dirty-dog belt past, both of them barking joyously, snapping and shirt-fronting as many sheep as they can, like thugs running amok in a church fete. I see Rowan leap after a stray, over-shoot the sheep, and hit barbed wire. He yelps once, gets up, and keeps running.

'Steady, dogs!' I yell. 'Steady!'

The dogs slow down, now trotting, a pink-tongued tag-team trio. Johnny is still yelling. At me? At Tiger? At Ralph? No, at Jeannie, the small brown kelpie.

Twenty metres ahead I see the boss propped in the stirrups, one arm outstretched as if it was a speargun.

'Go, Jeannie! Go! Speak!'

And go Jeannie does. She bounds across rounded sheep backs in four-paw drive, hits the ground running, dives through the fence, and streaks away like a little red rocket with a tail. She barks as she runs, short sharp noises that let the mob of breakaways know that they're in strife. Some stop, Jeannie passing them by, a missile on a mission in search of the leaders of the pack. And now I can see why Johnny's so concerned about turning our sheep back to the road.

Looking down the slope, on the far side of the smudge of green, are five hundred dim-witted merino country cousins all seeming quite interested at the prospect of a reunion with their long-lost relatives from down the track. If the two mobs get boxed, it'll take days to sort out.

'Drop the fence, Lal!' Johnny trots up on a business-like Bruce. 'I'm goin' through. Keep the wire flat. Stand on it. Kate, get up the front.'

Kate goes, I drop the fence and flatten the strands into the grass as Johnny comes through on Brucie, who snorts at me. Over the wire they go, their sights set on the two hundred troublemakers who Jeannie has now stopped dead in their tracks, eighty metres from the other, legal, residents. The boss turns to shout, a twisted wrinkle running up his shirt from hip to shoulder.

'Pick it up, Lal!'

I pick up the fence, straining so hard I think my child-bearing days are over even before they've started. Once it's vertical it's okay; I hold it, watching the broken-up flock on the road trying, like mercury tries, to join itself into one main blob.

'Keep it up!' Ralph yells. 'Or these other buggers'll hit it for six.'

I brace the fence as Ralphy takes the remainder of the flock past, the ewes panicking as Tiger worries at them from behind. I have to laugh. With his black-and-white face, gleaming teeth and extend-o tongue, he's the happiest-looking masked bandit ever to terrorise anyone or anything. He loves his job.

'Jeannie's got 'em,' Ralph informs me as Charlie tramples past. 'Looks like it, anyway.'

I turn to look. Jeannie has the sheep in a bunch, all facing outwards like settlers about to battle the Apache. Further up the hill, Farmer Brown's mob watch in utter amazement. If sheep could talk, they'd be saying 'my my, well, my goodness, well, hmmm, dear me'. But they can't talk, so they baa instead.

'Steady, Jeannie,' Johnny calls out, sitting stock still on Bruce, who the boss has positioned between the two mobs like a knight in a chess game. 'Walk up, go on, walk up.'

Jeannie walks steadily towards the runaways, who turn and warily begin to walk towards me and my collapsible fence. From red-alert, things have cooled down to medium-beige. Ralph and his lot have passed, Kate is leading the mob on with Rowan, Dirty-dog and Dusty-dog. The coast appears to be clearing. I lower the fence and retreat to take up a position down the track as a backstop. This manoeuvre earns me a wave from the boss.

'Stay there, Lal.'

I do, in the middle of the track, arms out, the top of my head hot in my hat, watching sheep and drovers and dogs. The day, it appears, has been saved – and I reckon I deserve a pat on the back almost as much as Jeannie deserves one on her head. Surely my scorecard's shot up at least one point on the Drover Scale. I feel sorry for Kate copping a blast, but she handled it in typical Kate Hart-style. She simply gritted her nice straight teeth, wiped her nose, and kept on going.

'Good job,' Johnny calls back to me.

Enough said. I see Rowan limping along, and call him over. Blood soaks his fur from shoulder to paw and has spattered back right along his side. There's a cut as long as a finger and as wide. I grab the dog by the collar and hold him.

'Hey, Johnny, come here for a minute. Quick.'

I'm sent to bring back Bett, some tools, and the first-aid box. This I do, and now that Rowan's been stitched up, strapped up, tied up, and given water, Johnny and I look at the fence.

'I'll cut a couple of posts,' Johnny says. 'You go and dig out the old two.'

I'm about to move when a red utility pulls up and out gets Farmer Brown. He's short, wide, blond-headed, about Johnny's age, tough-looking with a squashed nose. He walks slowly, his hands lost in the green depths of worn-out hard-yakka daks. Up and down the fence he looks, then again. He lets out a breath like a slashed tyre.

'I'd have to say,' he says, eye-balling Johnny, 'that she was just about cactus anyway.'

We stare at the fence resting in peace. Maybe, I'm thinking, we might be lucky. This bloke doesn't seem to have a particularly short fuse. Johnny's face is wrinkled with neighbourly sympathy, as if he'd helped build the fence with his own hands.

'Yeah, she's vergin' on the bad side of good,' he says, 'but we'll get her standing up again, since it was us who knocked her over.'

Since when, I want to know, have fences been female? At least Bett the truck has grease nipples and nice curves – but what's feminine about a fence? I decide that this is not the time to bring this subject into the open. Someone might think I'm mad.

Farmer Brown silently surveys the middle distance, where gum trees scratch blue sky with jagged branches. His sheep still watch us from the edge of the grass they don't seem to want to cross. We wait on words. Instead a hand that might've been hewn from a mallee root is put out to Johnny.

'Boot Thompson.'

Johnny shakes, introduces himself, and then indicates me.

'Lal Godwin there who works for me.'

We shake. Boot's a powerhouse, all right. My dad would've given anything to have him around when a piano needed to be lifted and shifted.

Boot Thompson takes out a stubby black pipe, stuffs brown weed into it, then lights it. The smoke's the same colour as his eyes. The match he blows out, snaps, rolls the bits between hard fingers, then grinds them into the dirt with his heel.

'It's still going,' I say, as a joke.

He looks at me. I shrug. 'Maybe not. Must've been my imagination.'

Boot changes the subject.

'You got some good dogs,' he says to Johnny, having decided that I'm only a helper, and perhaps not a very good one at that. 'That little red one saved your bacon, I'd say.'

Johnny agrees with the merest tilt of his hat. I can see Jeannie up ahead holding the mob, tirelessly trotting, scouting, delivering the occasional sharp yelp like a light smack.

'And now,' says Boot, rubbing his big paws together like a grizzly bear feeling the cold, 'if you could dig out those two snapped posts I'll get the couple of newies out of the ute and we'll be well on the way to having fixed up me good old fence.'

So we do, and with our help, he does.


Boot Thompson turns out to be a true gentleman and a scallop. Not only does he let Johnny bring the mob into a paddock that's whiskery with grass, he also invites the lot of us up to his place for a shower.

'A short shower,' he adds, then drives off up his snaky track towards a white, verandah'd house surrounded by a wild green hedge.

'And you need one, Kate,' I say, watching the red utility lay a dust screen across paddocks that fold into each other like creases in a fawn-coloured sheet.

'And you need two, Lal,' she says, the first words she's said since Johnny got stuck into her for going the wrong way.

'You witty old bag,' I reply, giving her a friendly elbow, dropping Bett's clutch, and with Ralph in the middle setting sail for the land of soap and some water.

Mistakes are strange and exotic animals. Some mistakes drive people apart forever – others work like magic glue. Kate's little blunder, I get the feeling, has united the lot of us. At least now we know the old moll's human!

# thirteen

We spend the day resting. With the sheep safely behind wire there's not a lot for drovers to do but wash clothes, tidy the truck, look after Rowan, plan my menu for the next couple of stops, and make the usual list of supplies that we'll need in the next day or so.

Having done all this, Kate finds me sitting in the shade, discussing with three-year-old Bronwyn Thompson why her cloth Snoopy dog cannot have pups. Bronny smoothes Snoopy's ragged ears with small square hands and tells her, or is it him?, not to worry about it.

'We've got other dogs,' she says. 'And sheep and cats. Lambs too, soon.'

I see Kate approaching, and do not need my sixth sense to tell me that she does not bear good news. She's dressed for riding, boots polished to shiny piano-brown.

'It's that time again, Lal,' she says ominously. 'And today we're going to learn how to trot. Let's saddle up.'

I deliver Bronwyn to her mum, Marlene, who's plonking away at a home computer in the cool of the kitchen, then walk back out into heat that hits me fair in the face.

I find myself perched on top of Aileen, who seems about as keen as I am about heading off around the block. I pat her neck, lean forward, and hint heavily that for well-behaved horses there are rewards.

'Cubes, Aileen,' I whisper. 'Handfuls.'

Aileen walks beside Massy, their hoofs clopping heavily, both of them smelling quite nicely of hay, grass, and horse. Kate explains the theory of trotting. She even shows me how to do it, moving off in front, her bottom going up and down, her voice at fifty decibels.

'Come on, Lal! It's easy!'

Whilst I'm deciding that we won't, Aileen decides that we will. Off we go, me being jiggled, bounced, and joggled. With great courage I try to copy what Kate does so easily, but succeed only in losing a stirrup and having the breath pounded out of me.

Kate stops, then trots beside, shouting instructions as if she's a mad conductor and I'm a tone-deaf, violin-murdering failure.

'Rise! And now! And now! And now!'

Through no talent or technique that I can claim as my own, I somehow find myself slotting into this Rising To The Trot business. It's a miracle! I've turned into Princess Anne!

'Hands down! Sit up! Elbows in! Bottom under!'

This last bit of advice I ignore and leave my bottom exactly where it has been for the last nineteen years of my life.

'Keep going, Lal!'

Hey, check this out! I've got the rhythm! I'm actually riding a horse – and apart from going a lot faster and me being a lot higher than I expected, it's not so bad. We trot downhill until we're under trees that meet overhead in a lattice of sparse leaves and bony branches. Kate slows Massy, who snorts and reefs at the reins for the hell of it.

'Walk, Lal,' says Kate, paying no attention to her performing horse, 'rein her in.'

Aileen slows to a walk immediately and again I pat her hot moist neck, trying to impart friendly vibes. As we pass under a low branch, Kate stands in her stirrups and plucks a gumleaf flyswat. She gathers reins into one gloved hand, making an arrangement as neat as a posy of flowers.

'Not bad, Lal. You'll get there.'

'Where, heaven?'

For fifteen minutes we walk the horses along the road, patches of hot dappled light drilling holes in the shadows. The afternoon seems timeless, a wide open space for thinking and quiet talking.

'Johnny's a good guy,' I say, 'isn't he? How come he's not married or something? I mean, he's sort of a bush Superman.'

Kate's gumleaves rattle and swish.

'He was engaged once. To a teacher. But the shearing kept him away for months and months, and in the end she just took off. Couldn't hack the waiting, I guess.' Kate tries to drive the flies away from the horses' ears. 'That flattened him for a while.'

My eyebrows push up the freckles on my forehead.

'I can't imagine anything'd flatten him.'

She shrugs. 'It did. So, you and Ralph? Are you guys, ah, together or . . .?'

'Well, nope,' I say. 'Good friends, but that's all. Now.'

'Oh, sorry, I mean I shouldn't have asked.' She even looks sorry.

'That's cool,' I say. 'I mean, the friendship-thing's cool anyway. It wasn't always. We had a few rough patches, but it's fine now. What about you?'

Kate's smile seems directed inward, as if she knows exactly what I'm talking about. Like, relationships are number one tricky business.

'Single,' she says, 'but yeah, it's complicated. I've made a few mistakes. Big ones, actually, but – ' She laughs. Obviously not that big. 'You meet someone, go out, go to – no, I haven't got a boyfriend at the moment. I'm resting. Gathering my strength.'

The way Kate talks makes me laugh. She pretends the world is all too hard for her, but I know she really knows it's not. I can't help liking people who admit they don't have all the answers, even though I think Kate has a few more answers than most. She's real. She's got a cold sore to prove it.

'Sometimes,' Kate says, her words dropping in amongst the clip-clopping of eight hoofs, 'some of the best things about my life are more like a trap. You know, the money, uni, car.' She looks at me. 'Everybody expects me to go in one direction. Get the degree, the job, the husband. Sometimes I'd prefer just to chuck it all in and be as free as you are.'

I nearly fall off the horse.

'Free?' I splutter. 'Me? Hell, I'm not free, geez, I just stagger from one thing to another.' I shake my head as if I'm seeing stars. I hold up fingers one by one. 'School drop-out, tuna factory, dole, pub job, boxing sideshow, this. Free?' I look straight up the dusty road. 'And then who knows what I'll – '

It hits me that this is a beautiful old road – stately trees and wholemeal-coloured hills on both sides. I get the feeling I've been sounding like a whinger.

'It's my own fault, I know,' I say, patting silver shirt buttons. 'I should've stayed at school and all that, but at the time – ' How do I explain all the things that were going on and the feelings I had back then? My head was driving me nuts.

'Tell me, Lal, go on.'

Okay, I will tell her.

'A friend of mine died,' I say, 'so I left school.' I try to think carefully about why I did what I did. 'Then I figured I didn't need school, because I thought I could beat the system by living this romantic, adventurous life. I thought – ' This is what I was thinking back then. 'I thought maybe the world might reward me for being brave. I thought I could travel and find cool jobs and have this kind of famous life, but it didn't quite happen.'

Kate laughs, a warm sort of a laugh that doesn't make me mad or show that she thinks she's got the drop on me.

'This is pretty cool though, isn't it, Lal?' Her hands and her head move to take in the road, paddocks, sky, hills. 'Pretty adventurous. Sort of romantic. Beats selling bowties or nylon underpants.'

I agree. This droving is good.

'I'm more worried about after this,' I add. 'Like what me and Ralph are going to do then.'

'That makes three of us,' Kate says. 'I don't know either. Sometimes law seems like it'd choke me to death. It's so kind of locked away, like a private madhouse.' She slumps, bra-strap ridging her back, then she straightens like a spring. 'Tell you what's funny, though – that both of us thought the other had it easy.' She chuckles, kicks Massy into a trot, and quickly leaves me behind. 'You'll be okay, Lal!' she yells back. 'You're too bad-tempered to put up with too much shit!'

What can I say? She's right of course. My life's fine. Mostly, anyway. Maybe Kate ought to be a psychologist rather than a lawyer? Maybe she ought to tie a string to her pocketknife? Because there it is on the track. Now how the hell do I go about getting down from here to get it?

*

It's knee-to-knee around the fire. Boot Thompson and family have joined us for the evening, but with our sheep not within cooee, the night sounds of talk, scrambling possums, crackling wood and shifting leaves seem only to half-fill the darkness. Boot, his pipe firing, asks Johnny where we're headed from here. Johnny, holding a tin cup of red wine, lets out names like favourite homing pigeons from a crate.

'Clifton,' he says. 'Bidgee Creek, Weerup, Clive, Dennington, home. Or thereabouts. Should give us a show for this rain that's supposed to be on its way. With a bit of luck.'

'Amen,' says Boot, rumbling, which I work out is his version of laughter. 'A bloke's gotta believe things'll get better, eh?' He pokes at the fire, a man who's not good at not being busy.

Marlene Thompson, holding Bronny who dangles sleepily like a ventriloquist's doll, appears to measure and weigh each word before she says them.

'You people oughta be proud of yourselves. Someone's got to put their foot down and say enough's enough.' She looks into the fire, like we all look into the fire, except Boot.

Boot slaps one big loggy leg and re-doubles his grip on his pipe.

'Here here.'

I sip my wine, tongue paddling around in its earthy coolness, whilst I try to work out why the name Dennington rings a bell. Denningon? Do I know Dennington? Bingo! Dennington's where shearers dance, where the beer's cold, and who-knows-who walks lonely bush roads after midnight.

I file the name in my memory box, figuring the more you know about things the less mysterious they become. Mostly, anyway.

# fourteen

I come barrelling around a corner, the injured Rowan on the seat beside me. There on the track, in blue shorts, white polo shirts, and sunglasses, are three blokes. I also spot a white station-wagon with the egg-shaped logo of Dubbo Television painted on the door. Could this be . . .? I hit the brakes. Hold on, Charlie-horse, we're stopping!

'Howdy,' I say, elbow out the window.

The biggest and smoothest-looking guy takes a step forward. He's tall, his shoulders extend an XL shirt, his hair's short and brown, and his sunglasses are Rayban Wayfarers – exactly like mine, except mine are $15 copies.

'Yeah, gidday,' he says, 'we're from Dubbo TV News, and we're trying to catch up with a bunch of drovers who are supposedly somewhere round here. You wouldn't know them or 've seen them, by any chance?'

'*Absolutement,*' I say. 'I'm one of 'em. I'm Lal Godwin, the driver. The others are up ahead somewhere with the mob.'

The guy snaps strong clean fingers. 'Great,' he says, but not all that enthusiastically. A hand is put out in the same way. 'I'm

Jeff Johanssen.' He gestures, a flat expensive-looking watch glinting, towards two other guys who are squatting in the shade lighting cigarettes. 'That's Knobs, my soundman, and Simon, often known as Sly, my cameraman. Wave, Simon.'

Simon, or Sly, is a lean, tanned, tennis-player type. He holds up a hand as if it was someone else's. I get the feeling I'm being sent-up gutless, but I don't show it. I don't wave back, either.

'Wave thank-you, Knobs.' The guy next to Bett holds his hands up as if he's conducting an orchestra, lets it fall.

The soundman's more the kind of guy you'd see fishing off the Delaney Bay pier late at night: stocky, choppy black hair, big freckles, a face as pale and plain as the underside of a pizza box.

'I'm Lal,' I call out. They don't care. They keep on smoking. Both are wearing coloured cord surfer bracelets.

'What we want to do, Lal,' says Mr Jeff, shielding his smoothly shaven and tanned face from the afternoon sun, 'is get some pictures of the sheep and the drovers, a short interview, then split. You're not the boss, are you?'

I admit I'm not – then I have a brainwave.

'Got a spare half hour?'

He stretches, lifting his arms, showing not even the tiniest wet patch.

'Sure. What's the plan?' He glances at his crew.

I put Bett into first and check my mirror. 'Follow me. Don't worry, I don't drive fast.'

'We do,' he says, motioning for his crew to move.

Simon and Knobs stand, flicking their cigarette butts onto the road.

'You better stamp on 'em,' I suggest out my window. 'We need a bushfire round here like a hole in the head.'

Knobs, the one who looks like a pizza box, walks to where his cigarette still smokes, and grinds it into the dirt.

Simon hops, steps, and jumps – then performs the Mexican hat dance purely for my benefit. He bows. I clap twice. Jeff drags out car keys from his pocket. I tell them that they'd better stay back a bit, or they'll be vacuuming the car for a week.

'Don't worry,' says Jeff, 'cleaning the car isn't our job. Stories are.' He grins like a pirate. 'And that's what we do, ma'am.'

I take off, the station-wagon prowling along behind like a ghost car in the rising clay-coloured cloud.

'Thanks, men,' I say, and hand out cordial by the bucketful.

Whilst they drink I survey the camp. We're in a dip by a black-holed creek, where skinny gums throw shadows onto long, lion-coloured grass. Black cattle gaze at us from behind barbed wire, the remains of hand-dropped hay staining the side of the hill. No Shooting signs hang, which really mean Keep Off, Keep Out, Keep Going. But we're not breaking any laws here. We're in the endless, timeless, precious freedom of the long paddock and we can stay in that paddock as long as we like.

The Dubbo television crew have grudgingly helped me gather wood, and with the help of Knobs, who seems a pretty good guy, I've taken a huge gamble and set up the brake. I point to the dusty white station-wagon catching its breath under a tree.

'That thing got air-con?'

Simon, who's lazily tossing stones for Knobs to hit with a stick, looks at me with amazement from under the brim of a purple baseball cap. Curly blond hair bubbles down and over his collar.

'Do we look like the kinda guys who'd leave home without it?' Toss, whack, gone.

They don't. They look like the kind of guys who are used to pushing buttons to make money, play music, cook food, and to keep cool – but that's fine with me today. I pile in the back with Knobs, Simon's in the front with Jeff, and poor old Rowan's been left chained to Bett's front bumper, a bucket of precious water his only companion.

As we cruise, a cool breeze straight from the Commodore factory does me the world of good. Knobs offers me a cigarette, which I politely knock back.

'Nah, I hate the bloody things.'

He and Simon light up and blow smoke at me. I flop back in the seat as far away from them as I can, and open the window.

'Hey, cowboy,' says Simon, 'stop letting the cool out.'

'And the dust in,' says Jeff, his voice debonair and smooth, as if he's very much aware of how he sounds. And likes it.

'And the flies,' adds Knobs. 'Keep 'em out. I hate flies. Out here they bite.'

I wind up the window, restoring the order of the crew's separate world. I tell them that it's not even all that hot today, then I ask them what happens when they actually do have to stop and go outside.

'We stand real still,' says Knobs, talking on behalf of the other two. 'Preferably in the shade. And hope all the action comes to us.'

They laugh, hanging loose. Nothing worries this bunch. They're being paid, heaps probably, to sit here, be cool, act cool, get a story, then go home. Good job!

'Normally we don't do this outdoorsy country and western stuff,' Jeff adds, steering with one hand low on the wheel. 'We do court stuff, the police beat, the odd car accident. Crime, mostly.'

'Murders make news, cowboy,' says Simon, tossing me a Mintie. 'Not sheep. Still, maybe we'll find an angle. We usually do.'

My Mintie is the runt of the litter. The pack has disappeared. Now I know why they call him Sly.

Jeff Johanssen has a pow-wow with Johnny and is told what he can do and where he can go – and where he can go if he breaks the rules. Jeff relays this information to his crew, and I stick around to make sure their car doesn't get in the way. Ralphy gives me a laid-back wave, slouched in the saddle, hat down, like a hall-of-fame stockman hero. Kate, I note, has retreated to the rear. Me, like most Aussies, I want to be on TV!

'Okay,' says Jeff, starting the station-wagon, keeping an eye on the moving mob behind us. 'Roll it, guys. Here they come.'

I look back, and I cannot help but think that these sheep are something special. Two thousand bobbing noses, nodding ears, kindling-stick legs, walking on under an inland sky that doesn't promise them much – but still they keep going.

Simon, sunglasses parked on top of his head, sits on the tail-gate with his camera, a gold chain slithering around his neck. Knobs, lying beside him, points a huge, furry microphone back at the sheep, as if he's about to wipe them out with a ray-gun. Jeff drives with two fingers hooked over the bottom of the wheel, muttering under his breath about dust and shimmer and angles. I sit next to him and eat the rest of the Minties.

Jeff's nodding now, pleased, watching his crew, watching the wide-spread flock, hardly watching the road at all. I take that job, as a head-on with a bullbarred ute can ruin your whole day.

The sheep are spread from fence to fence, stopping, starting, allowed to eat as much as they can. I see Jeff has spotted Kate and so has Simon, who is zooming in. Compared to Ralphy, Johnny and myself, she looks like she's been planted there by the director of a C-grade western.

'She's camera shy,' I whisper to Jeff, as I guess Knobs doesn't want my beautiful voice on his wonderful soundtrack. 'But don't let that put you off.'

The TV crew corner Johnny as he hobbles the horses. Knobs kneels, holding the microphone out on its pole, his gear held together by miles of silver tape. Simon, big black camera stuck to his eye, counts down, fingers disappearing into his fist.

'Five, four, three, two – ' Jeff hurriedly arranges his face.

'It's sundown,' he says, his voice controlled and pleasant, 'still a hot twenty-nine degrees and we're approximately two hundred kilometres north-west of Dubbo. With me now is Johnny Hart, boss drover, ex-shearer, and hopefully the saviour of these two thousand merino sheep. It's a tough assignment, John, isn't it?'

Johnny stands with his hands on his hips, his rigid calipered leg and worn-down boots making him look as unbending as a tree stump.

'Yeah, it's tough all right,' he says, but not like Jeff says it. He says it like he's swearing. 'We need rain more than anything now. The sheep are travellin' all right, but water's the problem. As you can see. Country's dryin' up fast.'

The paddocks around us are spiked with useless dead grass and scabbed with wide brown bare patches. Broken-down fences close in empty land.

Jeff nods, and as tall and big-shouldered as he is, he looks willowy compared to the boss. And as fresh from town as a crisp white shirt.

'There's a chance,' the news reporter says, 'this might not

turn out as you hoped, I guess. You can't stay on the road forever.'

Johnny's hat moves a fraction. He looks at the ground, his
face creasing and hardening.

'We go till we can't go no more.' He looks straight ahead,
up the winding track, then at Jeff. 'Then if the.sheep can't
travel, we stop, and then, yeah, we've had it. Until then we're
still in business.'

That's the longest speech I've ever heard Johnny make.

'What are the chances of rain, John?'

Our boss looks up at the yellowing afternoon sky, and sniffs.

'Not high. Not yet.'

'And choices, Johnny?' Jeff has his hands on his hips, his
head angled slightly forward. 'Do you have any?'

'Choices?' says the boss, as if he's been offered the hang-
man's noose or a lethal injection. 'Yeah, go or stop. But if it's
stop, then I guess I have the choice of shooting the sheep
myself, or have some other poor bastard do it for me.
Hopefully it'll rain before it comes to that.'

I notice the sound of the sheep in the brake. They sound
sad and pathetic and they look, against the harsh backdrop of
dry paddocks and stark gum trees, doomed. It won't rain. The
sky's hard as tin.

'I think all of Australia,' says Jeff, 'would join you in your
hope for rain, and wish you success with your journey. Jeff
Johanssen, Griddle Creek, outback New South Wales.'

Jeff thanks Johnny, they shake hands, then the both of
them walk off towards the brake, pointing and talking. I don't
follow them.

Instead I mosey on over to where Simon and Knobs have
instantly moved away to sit under a tree and drink cans of
mineral water. They look up, I sit down uninvited.

'Wanna drink?' says Knobs. 'There's heaps in the car.'

I shake my head. 'Nah, thanks, I'm okay.' I point at the big black Sony camera and sound equipment lying in aluminium boxes. 'So how'd you guys get jobs like this anyway?' If you could actually call what they do a job.

Simon smiles slowly at Knobs. I detect a trick serve about to come my way.

'You get my smokes from the car, I'll tell you.'

'And get us another drink, too,' adds Knobs, as he retapes a wire onto his microphone pole. 'Passionfruit or lemon.'

'Deal,' I say, and off I trot to the Commodore, thinking that this TV caper could be quite interesting, which is why I'm prepared to do a bit of grovelling.

I get Knobs a drink and pick up Simon's smokes, but I leave the lighter on the dashboard. Just call me Sly.

All of us stand around the fire drinking the Dubbo boys' mineral water, the crew about to split.

'Johnny,' says Jeff slowly, 'look, how's it sound if we were to come back a couple of times to check your progress?' His drink can he moves in an arc. 'I think this story's got some legs. I think people'll be really interested. I think you've got something pretty important happening here. Could we come back? That be okay with you and your team? We won't get in the way.'

Well. So now we're a serial, are we? Ralph, Kate and I wait on Johnny's answer. What could we call it? Drovers – Legends in Their Own Lunchboxes?

Johnny squats awkwardly and pokes at the fire. I know he's stalling, but of course Jeff doesn't.

'Ah, Jeff,' the boss says uneasily – poke, poke, flip, poke. 'Look . . . I suppose so. If you're not out to make us look like somethin' we're not. I guess a bit of publicity might show some of these buggers in Canberra how hard some people are doin' it in the bush.'

I'm flabbergasted, Jeff merely looks pleased.

'Terrific. We'll be no trouble, I guarantee it. It's a great story.' He finishes his can, crushes it, and throws it into the fire. 'We'd better go. These laddies get too much overtime as it is. Thanks, everyone. See you in a couple of weeks or so.'

Looks like TV time is over, this time. The Dubbo crew walk to their car and start to load their gear. Music from the Commodore flings alien sounds at the trees. Boxes are slid in and I see a scatter of cassettes on the front seat. Ralph hands Simon the last silver box. The cameraman stows it, brings down the rear window, then lights a cigarette. He offers Ralph one, and laughs at me.

'Where you guys from?'

'Me? Delaney Bay,' I say. 'Two hundred kilometres below Wollongong. The beach. Where they don't smoke. Don't go there.'

'Too late, mate.' He does Groucho Marx with his cigarette. 'Been there already. Good waves. Surfed it a few times. Nice point break. How 'bout you, Ralph? Same story?'

Ralphy shakes his head. 'Nah, down south. Victoria.'

Simon draws in smoke and blows it out in a thin stream.

'Yeah? Victoria's a big place, mate.'

Ralph nods. 'Me family are on the river. The Murray. Up Barmah-way. A couple'a places really. Moved around a bit.'

It occurs to me that Ralph's being cagey. Simon doesn't seem to notice, although he seems happy enough to play a kind of guessing game.

'Barmah anywhere near Swan Hill, Ralph. Or Echuca? We get down there a bit.'

I sniff casually, flick the end of my nose with a knuckle. Maybe I should try for a change of subject?

'Where are you from – ' Too late.

'I went to school in Echuca,' Ralph says. 'For a while.'

Simon gets into the Commodore. The window is wound down, a hand holding a cigarette is held out.

'Me and the boys were there last year.' Simon taps ash. 'Some dude turned up dead in the river. Tied with fishing line and with a big bump on his head. Cops never pinged anyone for it, but. You hear about that, Ralph?'

A sliver of fear inserts itself between my ribs.

'Can't really remember it,' says Ralph steadily, 'lotta people drown in the Murray.'

'When'd it happen?' I ask, acting dumb. 'Just recently?'

Simon, his cigarette now between his teeth, draws the seat-belt out and down. I hear it click home.

'Nah, six, seven months ago. Coppers are still workin' on it.' He tucks his shirt in, slumps back like a rock star in a limo, talks from the shadows. 'I'll check it out for you when we get back to work.' The Commodore starts, Simon lifts a hand. 'Give you the drum next time. Catch ya, cowboys. Take it easy.'

We watch the white Commodore disappear into the dark, heading back to Dubbo. Ralph and I don't say a word.

Diary.

4th April

Weather: clear, pretty warm.
Coota Lake (puddle).

The TV guys have come and gone like the wind — and like the wind they've stirred things up a bit. By tomorrow night our sheep will be walking through nice cool lounge rooms with us right behind them. Whoops, sorry about the carpet, folks! But it's all in a good cause. Like, our survival.

The TV guys — well, Sly Simon — also managed to kick all those sleeping dogs I was happy to let lie. I wasn't ever going to mention the Echuca-thing again to Ralph, but I have to now.

Look, no matter how close you are to someone, you can never know all there is to know about them. Ralph, compared to Em, has always remained a bit of a mystery to me. Em and I grew up together. We went to the same kinder, same school, same beach, same just about everything. I understood her, she understood me.

Ralph's different, for quite a few reasons. His feelings for the river and the red-gum forests go so deep it'd take more than words to explain. It's hard to tell someone about a place where your heart and soul belongs, where the whole land speaks to you, and even the very sounds are yours.

With Ralph it's what he can't tell me that is the most important part of what he feels. After all, no one can explain forty thousand years of his-tory or things that are inborn. But Ralph does have to tell me if there's something important I don't know about the body-in-the-river thing, otherwise we'll be finished. Friendship is only a small boat. Hidden secrets can sink it like the sharpest of rocks. That I do know.

# fifteen

Three dusty days go by, each hotter than the last. I reckon I've never seen anything so still as these huge paddocks sweltering in the heat. Nothing moves. Sheep huddle in puddles of shade, a windmill stands like a dried flower, the grass crackles and fence lines stagger off into the haze. And every day now Johnny carries the rifle with him in a leather boot strapped beside his saddle. And uses it, a sharp *crack!* that splits the hot air as he finishes off a sheep that can't go any further. On the radio I hear wool and sheep prices are still going down.

From the back of Bett I take a folding chair, unfold it, and sit. The camp's set up and I'm sitting here drinking orange cordial, waiting for someone to roll up to help me with the brake.

'Whose bright idea was this anyway?' I ask Jeannie, who looks at me from where she's neatly curled beneath the red-topped card table. She wags her tail once, without the power to turn over a gumleaf.

\*

I insist that Ralph and I take turns with the sledgehammer. He shrugs and hands it over. I whack a post in and Ralph holds it low down, smart comments floating out from under his hat.

'Nearly hit it that time, Lal. Beaudiful, two in a row. Keep goin' while you're hot, kid.'

'I'd shut up if I were you,' I say, stopping to wipe sweat off my face. 'I haven't got a very good grip.'

We move in a semicircle, hammering, sweating, swearing, kicking sticks out of the way, keeping an eye out for snakes. I can't remember being so hot for so long as the last couple of weeks. We talk less and less, saving our breath, and all of us look dirtier and tougher and wilder by the day. Out here is not the place, I'm learning, to wear your heart on your sleeve. You just say what you've got to say, then shut up. Beating around the bush takes too much energy.

Ralph and I finish the brake and go back to the camp. In the shade we sit and take turns to guzzle from a battered foam drink container.

'Okay,' I say straight out, after we've cooled down, 'tell me everything about the night you had a blue with this bloke by the river. Maybe you've missed a bit out, I think.'

Ralph's answer is to shoot a nasty look at me, and then another up the track. Sorry, mate, no sign or sound that the sheep are coming, only the empty dusty road curving between trees with bark hanging off them like stiff brown bandages. I figure I've got about five minutes at the most before the mob arrives.

'Were you by yourself that night?' I add, plunging on. 'Or were you with someone else? You don't often go fishing alone, do you, Ralph?' I pick up a small stick and fiddle with it, not looking at him as I roll it between my fingers. 'Come on, Ralphy, I have to know.' Ralph also looks at my stick as I twirl it one way then the other.

'I was by meself in the fight,' Ralph says quietly. 'I already told you that.'

'But before or after, you were . . .?' The words prop in the still air, refusing to go away. Ralph pulls at the rough ponytail he's bundled his hair into.

'Earlier on I was fishin' with the Riverman. He's an old hermit-bloke who lives on the river. Got a boat, goes way upstream and down. He don't live nowhere, camps anywhere.' Ralph takes a slow breath. 'When I was walkin' back to the road from his place I run into the other fella – the one with the fishin' lines. He was coming from his ute through the trees, carryin' lines and beers and crap. He knew he'd been sprung doing what he bloody shouldn't have been doin'.'

This place that Ralph comes from – his country, the river and red gum forests – it must be so different from Delaney Bay. Delaney Bay's open, bright, and busy. Mostly it's a happy joint, full of holiday people. Ralph has told me what it's like out in the forest. He says the quietness of the place, the feeling of it, is so strong it seems to hug you. He says the river doesn't make a sound, but you can hear it anyway.

'This Riverman, Ralph, does he have a proper name?'

Ralph eyes me. 'Yeah. Riverman. What's wrong with that?'

I stammer. 'Yeah, but no, he wouldn't call himself that, though, would he?'

Ralph scrapes up a handful of grey dust and crushes it in his hand. He drops it, a shell-shape, and watches it break open. I fiddle with my stick, feeling uneasy.

'He doesn't call himself anythin',' Ralph says. 'He don't talk about much, except about the river, and when he's got something important to say. Not like you, Lal.'

I carry on regardless. 'So, like, what's he live on?'

Ralph looks at me as if I'm sillier than he thought.

'The river. He fishes and hunts. Maybe he might swap you a couple'a yellowbellies for a couple'a dollars or somethin' like that, but not often. I always give him a stubby or two. He doesn't mind a beer. Tell you a good story for a beer. Told me one about the last of the paddle steamers took the wool down in 1957.'

I can hear the sheep now. To me, at this moment, they sound more like a distant pack of hounds closing in. I drop my stick and swivel right around to face Ralph.

'So when you left the guy you hit, Ralph, he was alive and not in the river?'

Ralph looks at me angrily. 'I told you yes a hundred times, Lal. How many more times d'you have to hear it?'

I move closer to Ralph, reaching out, my hand on his arm.

'Maybe the Riverman might've had a fight with this guy later? Over the fish or something?'

'Maybe he did,' says Ralph, pushing my hand away, standing up, beating dust off his jeans. 'And if he did, good luck to him. Someone's gotta protect the river and the things livin' in it.' He walks away, stopping in the middle of the track, turning. 'If someone's stealin' from you, who knows what you do?'

I follow Ralph. 'Ralph, is this Riverman a whitefella or a blackfella?'

Ralph stops. The sheep come into sight, spread right across the track, from fence to fence, floating on dust.

'What d'you reckon, Lal?'

'Ahm, blackfella.'

Ralph works at fitting his hat to the right downward sloping angle.

'Whitefella. What's it matter anyway?' He pokes a hand roughly in my direction. 'Don't ask me any more about it.' Ralph walks off, a slim straight-backed figure in the blazing sun.

I stay near the camp, but move into a position where I can help drive the sheep into the brake. I keep looking at Ralph, but he never looks at me, the sheep flowing between us like a living river. I concentrate on the job, but I can't help thinking it'd be interesting to talk to this Riverman, for quite a few reasons.

For three days we stop while Johnny does some shearing. The property we're on is enormous. Running right through it is a fenced three-kilometre long track, and this is where we put the mob. So, we wander with sheep, taking it in turns to check on them, plodding in pairs on the horses through the days like coppers pounding the beat. I ride Aileen, the pair of us qualifying as the world's slowest and most careful horse and rider.

Each morning Johnny leaves camp, carrying a canvas waterbag and a towel. And each morning he reminds us that the sheep are our responsibility. Then he walks away, heading for the big grey tin woolshed on the hill, leaving one thousand nine hundred and ninety-odd merino ewes in our care. And that's a lot of sheep.

In the cool of the morning Kate and I decide to walk out to the mob, which is bottled in a laneway not far from camp. We leave Ralph sitting under a tree reading a five-day-old newspaper.

'Rain?' Kate says, checking out the overcast sky as she stuffs a spare hayfever-suitable hanky into her jeans pocket.

The one thing she never forgets is her hanky, but today I don't think she'll need it. The air flows over my bare arms like water. No sign of a north wind. To feel cool is almost as refreshing as having a shower. Almost.

'Looks a bit hopeful,' I say, doubt edging into my voice, because the land seems close to exhaustion – and even though the day's not going to be hot, cicadas still sing their pitiless songs. They've seen it all before I guess, up there in their leafy hideaways. They don't care how dry it is or how merciless the weather; they'll always survive, us and the sheep might not.

'How's Johnny handling it, you reckon?' I ask. 'Like, underneath it all?'

Our boots hardly make a sound in the sandy lizard-tracked soil.

'He's okay, I think,' Kate says slowly, 'but the one thing he can't stand is to see the sheep copping it. If it does get bad, I mean really bad – ' She stops, reaches up to pluck a gumleaf flyswat, looks at me, then walks on again. 'He won't push them until they fall over. He'd shoot them first.'

I nod. Things seem more straightforward when it's not hot. They mightn't actually be any better, but they seem clearer. Your thoughts go in lines. Either it rains or it doesn't. And if it doesn't, and we can't get the mob in on water, *finito*. Simple.

'We just keep on keepin' on,' I say. 'As if things are okay, don't we?'

'Yeah.' Kate slows a bit, measuring out her steps, putting her heels down first. 'Johnny's human though, Lal. It is possible to cheer him up. He's not indestructible. He can't do it all by himself. It doesn't hurt to gee him up a bit every now and again.'

We walk up the narrow lane, the sheep moving off in panicky groups, sticks crackling under their small hard hoofs. They seem all right, the silky fleece of their noses looking like suede, their eyes bright as marbles and as crazy-looking as usual.

'Thank God we didn't find any down,' I say. 'I hate it when they're shot. The sound's awful, like they've been smacked across the forehead with a cricket bat.'

Kate doesn't say anything. She looks around, hands on her hips. She can use the rifle, Kate. I've seen her work the bolt, shoot a can off a stump, send the empty cartridge flickering away like a wasp.

'Well, they all look all right,' she says. 'Not too bad.' She blows her nose, more experimentally than anything, to see how her nostrils are performing, then stuffs the hanky into her jeans. 'Hey, what was that Simon guy saying about a body in the river at Echuca?'

My hand jerks up as if I'm trying to block the question, but I recover quickly enough to make sure I don't give her any reason to think there are lots of beans to be spilled. I outline the bare bones of the story, so to speak. Ralph I hardly even mention – not that Kate would ever say a word to the TV guys. She wouldn't, because like a good lawyer, she knows exactly when to keep her mouth shut.

Diary.

*7th April*

*Weather: Cool, grey, lovely.*
*Daggar Station.*


*Today Ralph, Kate and I sat around polishing boots and mending clothes. Ralph was talking about the teams of Aboriginal shearers there used to be in the bad old days. Hardly got paid, he reckoned. The station-owners gave them clothes, smokes and tucker, but no money. Of course it's different now, with the union having put a stop to dodgy crap like that.*

*I'm sure Ralph would make a good shearer. And if he could get himself a job where he'd be working side by side with people, rather than slugging it out toe to toe with them, that'd be great. Shearers get paid for what they*

124

*do and how good they are. I bet Ralphy would learn fast.*

*I hope Dell's okay back at Barramah. When you're on your own, trouble, like money trouble, can feel totally overwhelming. And when one person's trying to keep a dream going that two people used to share, it really is twice as hard. Dell won't cave in, though. She and Johnny'll get Barramah up and running. Or they'll die trying.*

*I think about Em. That girl's in my heart forever. Sometimes I can imagine her so clearly she could be right beside me. I'll try to do what I used to tell her I would. I won't sink without a trace. I'll bob around the place like a bloody beach ball! After all, one day Em and I might meet up again – and I'd hate to have to tell her I was a shocking piker.*

And now I'm going to bed. Immediately.

## sixteen

I am half-awake and somehow my face is half-wet. Possums? No, it is actually really and truly raining!

Softly, sparsely, one drop per gumleaf, water is magically falling from the blackness, making a sound like a million whispered blessings. Rain. I lie listening to it, letting it touch down on my face, each droplet leaving a small, cool point.

In silence, not a branch stirring, the bush absorbs water and I wonder what the arrival of rain might mean. How much water does grass need to grow and keep on growing? A fair bit I guess, but even as I think this it's as if the volume control has been turned to High. I sit up, then get up. There are things to be done and, in an oilskin miraculously found in the back of Bett, I do them, followed around by the dogs.

I shut Bett's windows, make sure saddlery and food boxes are totally covered, and bundle up a few shirts that have been washed. In the brake the sheep are commenting to each other about the turn in the weather, but they don't sound panicky or restless, so I leave them alone and go on poking around the camp.

'Lal.' It's Johnny, coming out of the dark, in jeans and boots, following a torch beam. 'This is nice,' he says quietly. 'Very nice.' He inspects his watch. It's five a.m. 'Might as well boil the billy.' He kneels to pull dry sticks from the bottom of the pile.

With a bit of newspaper he re-lights the fire, coaxing flames. We stand listening and watching as the fire gradually overcomes the damp until it starts to sizzle and crackle. For once there is no dust and everything smells fresh and woody. I remember the talk Kate and I had sitting on the log.

'We're gonna be okay now, I reckon,' I say. 'This is just the start of our good luck. Maybe it'll rain for weeks.'

Johnny squats, empty-handed, wet-shouldered, boots screwed into the damp earth.

'Yeah, we'll see, Lal. Day at a time. A good start, but.'

In cool saturating drizzle we strike camp. Everything is made harder by the rain but no one complains. Wet grass soaks my boots, horses shake heavy manes, the dogs slouch around unhappily on muddy paws. I stash the swags, olive-green canvas smeared with yellow clay, and the land as far as I can see has changed from the colour of gold to the colour of tin. We are all happy. A low-level joy runs through us like a weak electrical current that occasionally causes a spark.

'Send her down, Hughie!' Johnny calls up at the hanging grey belly of cloud. 'Another three days of this and we can turn for home.'

I give the boss the thumbs-up and slide a crate of cooking gear into the back of Bett. It would be good to be able to turn for Barramah knowing things were on the up and up. Like the grass.

Kate, poetically draped in her riding coat, trots past on slick, black Massy.

'Galloping this afternoon, Lal,' she calls out cheerily, then whistles Tiger and Jeannie, who prick up ears and pick up paws. 'Have a nice day.' She trots off to where the sheep are pouring from the brake, a knobbly stream that jostles and jumps as it flows.

Oh, great. Galloping is the horse equivalent of a jet breaking the sound barrier, only more dangerous. I toss the last of the swags into old Bett, wondering if planes are safer than horses, or if horses are safer than planes.

I'm struggling to set up the brake solo when a white DTV 5 station-wagon skids to a halt on the track. One long horn blast blows magpies from the trees, a hand waves from a window. Jeff, Simon and Knobs get out and wander towards me through the tall, normally papery grass, but today it's damp. Knobs trails a hand, knocking drops off the tops of the tallest stalks.

'We brought you the wet weather,' says Jeff. 'Told you we're nice fellas.' He breathes in deeply, looking around at the drip-drying trees.

'Knew you were good for something,' I say, happy to rest, letting the hammer slide down to the ground. 'How'd we look on the news? Cool, I hope?'

'Yeah, cool enough,' says Knobs, cupping hands as he lights up. 'Top story. The station got a heap of calls about it. Bet your boss is happy with the rain.'

Simon works at making tracks in the mud with a big pair of suede boots he's got on. He stomps along like an overgrown kid, then stops, as if he's been told to.

'You guys'd better make the most of these puddles,' he says, 'because the weather map doesn't look so good. There's a dirty big high comin' that's gonna cook the place. Thirty-nine in Perth yesterday. Bad news.'

Bad news, all right. And trust Simon to tell us. I don't think he gives a stuff about us really – all we're good for is to provide him with a few funky pictures.

'Thanks for tellin' me,' I say. 'Why don't you go and do something useful, like bang in a few stakes?'

'For you, Lal – ' He talks, a grin twitching, pointing at me like I was a target. 'Anything.'

I offer the heavy hammer. He taps it with a clean finger.

'But that. Sorry, I've got – ' He backs away, still playing. 'To shoot pictures of the old ute.'

Yeah, sure. Knobs takes the hammer.

'I'll do it. What d'you want me to smash the shit out of?'

Jeff, Knobs and I put up the brake. It's not such a hard job when there's three of us, the ground's a bit soft, and the weather's cool. In fact, it's quite good fun. We muck around and talk, me giving them my ideas on what they should shoot and questions they should ask. They mostly laugh, but when I tell them I want Jeff to introduce us by saying, 'Here we are out west with Johnny Hart's Heroes,' he rests the hammer on top of the last post and tells me he will.

'That's good, Lal. I'll use it.'

'Steal it, actually,' says Knobs, looking disappointedly at his biceps which are pale, freckly, and not all that big.

'Same thing,' says Jeff, and gives me back the hammer. 'Anything to beef up a story. Gonna boil the billy for us, Lal?'

'You've got arms,' I say. 'You do it.' It's a funny thing with Jeff; he looks as big and fit as a footballer, but he acts more like a movie star. I guess he is a kind of star, in a small way.

Jeff lets Knobs have a playful slap. 'Nah, Knobsy'll do it. Won't you, mate?'

'What'd your last slave die of?' I ask. 'Overwork?'

Jeff looks offended. 'Die? Nah, we sacked her. She didn't like how we went about getting some of our stories, did she, Knobs? Come on, Lal, I'll carry the hammer. Just to show I'm not a complete wanker.'

'Carrying a hammer won't prove much,' I say, and off we go, towards the fire and Simon, who is actually kneeling in the wet grass taking photographs of Bett with a flash-looking camera.

'Hey, Lal, I'll need you over here in a sec,' Sly says, as if he's a cook and I'm a side salad. 'Some shots for my private collection.'

Simon's a hard guy to work out. Sometimes I don't think he cares about anyone – but then surely a good cameraman must like people a bit, otherwise why would he want to spend his whole life shooting pictures of them? I walk over to where he's kneeling. Bett faces us front-on, like a black buffalo about to charge.

'You've got thirty seconds,' I say.

'Get in the old crate,' he says. 'You kind of match the whole thing.'

I get in Bett and hang my naked elbow out the window.

'Don't get too pushy, sport,' I suggest delicately, 'or I'll knock ya rotten.'

I generously make everyone billy tea, and drop in a few gum-leaves just for good measure. Jeff settles back, sips, then spits all over Knobs's new tennis shoes.

'That stuff's disgusting!' He wipes his mouth with the back of his hand.

Simon and Knobs stare into their mugs uneasily. I swirl mine around, then tilt it up.

'Why d'you think I'm drinking coffee?'

I dilute the tea until it becomes drinkable, then we get down to serious television business.

'This time,' Jeff says, folding up the sleeves of a shirt so new it has creases across the elbows, 'we're going to talk to you, Kate, and Ralph as well as Johnny. Director of News reckons the interest in this story's amazingly high.' He looks at me over the rim of his mug with light brown, almost honey-coloured eyes. 'Our timing was perfect. You guys seem to have struck a chord with all them good old folks at home.'

Knobs scrubs at his hair with his fingers. No wonder it sticks up.

'Yeah, it's kind of nice to deal with something positive for once.' He squints, his pale cheeks squashing up towards his eyes. 'Normally the people we go after are either in handcuffs or shooting at the coppers with rifles.'

Simon brushes off half a leaf that's stuck to his sock. He has a great talent for staying clean, that guy. I don't know how he does it.

'Yeah,' he adds, 'normally we're chasing the same idiots as the police are. People love to hate the bad guys.' He pulls a packet of chewing gum from his tartan-patterned shorts. 'As they say, you got a siege, you got a story.'

Jeff gets up, knee bones clicking. 'Yeah, there's nothing like getting close to a mental case with a gun.' He walks towards the Commodore, turning to talk as he walks backwards. 'Hey, Lal, if we need to test a few questions or get a bit of background info, you'll be around, won't you? Save us wasting Johnny's time, eh?'

'Sure,' I say. 'Yeah, it's best to keep out of his way.'

'Ex-cell-ent.' He goes to the station-wagon, opens the door and tosses out three green sausage-shaped parcels. 'Anybody out there know how to put up a tent?' he calls back to us. 'Because I certainly don't.'

From the station-wagon, from the silver boxes, the TV boys assemble their gear and troop over to where Johnny's waiting, holding Bruce's greasy bridle. Rather than a TV crew, our scared-of-nothing boss looks like he's about to face a firing squad. I don't think Johnny Hart's much of a public speaker.

Jeff outlines what he's going to ask Johnny whilst Knobs twiddles dials, his boom mike sticking out in front of him like a fishing rod with a big feather duster on top. Simon, with his camera, moves smoothly, gliding to a stop when he seems happy with the angle.

'Everyone set?' Jeff stands with Johnny, the camp and brake as the background.

Knobs, headphones on, nods. Simon's splayed right hand pokes out. His voice sounds a bit splashy, because he's still chewing gum.

'Four, three, two and – '

'We're here again in the north-east of New South Wales with Johnny Hart and his crew of battling drovers, whom I think you'd have to call heroes. At last it has rained and it seems that John and his team are about to circle back to Barramah Downs, where the mob set out from.' Jeff looks away from the camera to Johnny, who waits nervously, trying to find a place for his hands. He ends up crossing his arms.

'John, this is an heroic journey and it seems luck might have finally swung your way. Looking three hundred kilometres down the track, what would you see as the perfect end to this long and hard drive?'

'For a start, Jeff,' says Johnny drily, 'you can forget the bit about bein' heroes, but thanks for the thought.' He toes the ground with a battered boot, then looks past Jeff to where paddocks absorb the light rain that's falling. 'Look, from my great grandfather down us Harts've always been shearers. And we've always been, and will always be, union people. From the strikes of the 1890s right through we've always believed in a fair go for everybody.'

Johnny, I get the feeling, is beginning to like the idea of getting a few points across to an audience.

'So for me the perfect end to this droving trip would be if my sister Dell and I could get Barramah Downs up and running well. Then we'd be able, I hope, to start a chain that'd mean quite a few people right down the line'd earn a fair wage. That's how I see it. That'd be the perfect end, if it happens.'

Johnny and Jeff stand in the middle of the dreary afternoon, water sliding off their hats. Dripping gum-trees add background music. It's hard to believe that more hot weather is on its way.

'People think I'm mad for taking this mob out on the road,' the boss adds unasked, looking along the wet country road, 'but in a world fulla people who need clothes and food, two thousand sheep have gotta be worth more alive than dead, don't they? Geez, surely they do.'

Jeff nods, thanks Johnny, and tells his guys to cut. Simon, I see, doesn't stop shooting, but instead follows Johnny with his camera as the boss leads the small white horse away towards the brake, a hard man in a ten-year-old coat who's just tempted fate by talking about a perfect ending.

Walking, trotting, cantering – hold the phone! I bring Aileen back to a sedate stroll.

'Look, Kate –'

'Shut up, Lal, and listen. You can do this.' Kate's mother is an English teacher. She must've taught Kate the voice.

'I can?' I say doubtfully. 'I mean, I can. What about puddles?'

'It's uphill, Lal, Aileen won't go fast. She can't. Right, let's go!'

So, we go-o-o-o-oh! And the world goes galloping by-y-y-y-y! I think I just broke the sound barrier.

Diary.

12th April

*Weather: beautifully drizzly.*
*Deep Creek.*

*I've ridden a galloping horse. Which goes to show you can do something even if it scares the hell out of you. Once, of course, is enough.*

*Sometimes I really do feel as if I've got the rough end of the pineapple with this droving caper. I cook, clean, drag in wood, dig toilet holes, light fires, pack up – and the others just walk along behind the sheep whistling to the dogs and chatting to the neighbours.*

*Don't get me wrong, I still like it, being part of everything – but when I look at the TV guys zooming around making stories, digging and filling in toilet holes loses a fraction of its attraction. Still a job's a job and truly, this one's a good one. Apart from dunny duty.*

*I think Simon's right about the heat coming back. The sky's clear and the air's steamy. Just what we don't need; but the one thing no one can change is the weather. The one thing I can change, though, is how I think about myself. I'm okay. I've ridden a flying horse. I've got stuff to offer. I may not be the brightest, best-looking babe in the world, but I've got a feeling that maybe you don't have to be . . .*

# seventeen

At lunchtime Ralph, Kate and I are herded together by the TV crew. We're made to sit around the fire with three of the dogs and Jeff, who's going to ask us a few questions. Of course we are to be drinking tea, and the sheep, boxed up in a short lane, must plainly be heard. We sit.

'Three, two, one,' says Simon, and suddenly it's our turn to be stared at by Simon's camera and eavesdropped on by Knobs's fluffy mike.

Jeff is suddenly all business.

'Kate, Lal and Ralph. You've been droving for over a month now and have travelled over three hundred kilometres. Obviously you all get on well. I understand your backgrounds are all quite different?'

Silence, until I open my big trap.

'Yeah, I'm from the coast – ' I point to my grubby white singlet. 'Ralph's from Echuca on the Murray and Kate's from Sydney, the North Shore. But we don't hold that against her . . . much.' I look at Kate, whose nose is twitching. I hope she sneezes. She doesn't.

'Once you're out here,' Kate says slowly, not sure whether to look at the camera, Jeff, or me, 'it's how you work, not where you come from or what you wear. And besides, it's too hot to argue. And Johnny doesn't like arguments anyway, so we don't have any.'

Jeff accepts her comment, then adds another.

'I'd say this droving team is the perfect working model of how Australia ought to be. Different people from different backgrounds all working towards the one goal. Although your boss didn't agree, this droving of two thousand sheep is an heroic task. It's a tough business.'

'Heroes?' says Ralph. 'We aren't heroes, mate, we're just doin' the job for our wages.' He won't look at Jeff, but plucks at grass down by his boot. 'And we just try not to let the others down.' He glances at me, I nod at him.

Jeff's head and hand gestures show that he agrees.

'Would you say that perhaps these sheep might actually represent something special? That they're a symbol? That their survival, if they survive, might mark a turning point not only for Johnny, but for many other people as well? Australia-wide, even?'

Now that's a big question.

'They might be,' I say carefully, 'but – '

Kate cuts in. 'Whether or not our sheep make it – but they will – people in the bush will keep on going for absolutely as long as they can.'

'Yeah,' says Ralph, 'they're a tough mob.' He smiles slowly, his hands rising. 'The people we've seen out here, they'll hang on. They've helped us, too. Sometimes they let us have water and grass, and given us stuff they could've used themselves.'

'At the end of the day,' says Jeff, 'it all comes down to money, though, doesn't it? How long can people hang on 'til things get better? How much feed can they buy? How long can you stay out on the road?'

True, true and true. I begin to open my mouth, but Ralph opens his first.

'We can stay out here for six bloody months. We're gonna get this mob home no matter what. We'll work for nothin' if we have to.'

'Fair go, Ralph!' I say, talking to Jeff and the camera whilst I pat Ralph on the back. 'This fella's been out in the sun too long. We're not stayin' out for six months, I can tell you that. Or I'm not. Not for a million bucks, let alone nothing.' Kate puts her hand up in the air.

'Me neither. Two months max, then I'm gone. Johnny and Ralph can stay, though. They'd be quite happy to stay for twenty years. Without a shower.'

'Without any decent toilet paper,' I add, which gets Kate laughing, although she's trying hard not to by keeping her mouth clamped tightly shut.

'Without new undies,' I add, hoping that she'll let go a snotty snort and embarrass herself right across New South Wales.

Kate's battling to keep a straight face – then suddenly we're both laughing like Year 3 girls talking about a teacher's big fat bum. As can be plainly seen, your sense of humour tends to become pretty basic out in the sticks.

Kate and I laugh and keep on laughing. The wheels have fallen off the interview, especially since even Jeff's laughing now. And so's Ralph, and Johnny, and Knobs. Only Simon's still doing his job properly, and he yells, 'Cut it!'

But none of us do. It feels too good.

After the interview we eat sandwiches, try to find a decent piece of fruit out of the box, and fight over what's left of the chocolate. Simon, who's been quiet, suddenly throws a spanner into the works.

'Hey, Ralph, I found out a bit more about that body in the river down at Echuca.'

'Oh, yeah?' Ralph says casually, and spits a chunk of orange peel into the fire. 'What?'

I give up my battle with Kate for the last two squares of Fruit and Nut to hear what Simon has to say. He lobs a half-eaten apple off into the bush.

'Yeah, they're saying there was some blackfella down at the river around the time this dude got donged. But no one can find him. And they also reckon some old hermit bloke on the Murray might have a few clues about what happened – but no one knows where he's got to, either.'

'Who's "they"?' I ask, trying not to sound too interested. 'Scotland Yard or Derryn Hinch?'

Simon turns his sunglasses in my direction.

'A few people down there. The coppers have heard a few things, but it's not as if they're hammering wanted posters to trees. It's just a bit of talk I get from the, ah, bush telegraph, you might say.'

Ralph fishes a soggy bee out of the billy and flicks it.

'They can't be trying too hard to find these guys,' he says coolly. 'Echuca ain't a big town. Everybody knows everybody. And people along the river'd know this hermit fella, wouldn't they? Bit hard to hide for him too.'

Simon sits with his collar up, fingers drumming lightly on his knee. His grey eyes are as keen as a hawk's.

'Perhaps it's harder to find someone if the people around the place think that maybe he shouldn't be found.'

Ralph shrugs. 'Maybe, but the cops'd catch up with 'em sooner or later. Unless the fella on the river took off up a little creek or something.' He looks at Simon. 'Not many places to hide in Echuca. Unless maybe a bloke jumps in the river and stays there with a reed up his nose, like Tarzan.'

I chuckle at that, then move into the conversation, trying to sound relaxed and only half-interested.

'Do they really know this guy was murdered anyway? I mean, a bloke muckin' around at night in the Murray – hell, who knows what can happen?'

Simon stares at me now. I'm sure he only thinks in terms of pictures and news stories.

'Yeah, who knows, Lal? Who knows?' He stands up and walks, still talking, to where his camera rests in its aluminium box. 'It's an interesting story, but. A poacher with a bump on his head. A hermit on the river. A mysterious young blackfella. Yeah, it's all interesting stuff.' He kneels, watch flashing, lifts his camera onto his shoulder, and walks off up the road. 'I'm gonna shoot a few pictures,' he calls back to Jeff. 'There's a couple of dead trees up here that look pretty cool.'

We finish our lunch, I pack up, and in fifteen minutes the mob's back on the track. The TV guys load their gear and tell me they'll see us again closer to Barramah. I wave then drive away, passing Simon beside the track as he shoots a final shot of me and Bett, tracking us with the black Cyclops eye of his camera. I give him the finger and laugh, and make like it's a joke.

Under our boots the dirt once again turns to dust. The sun hangs over an orange horizon. The sheep in the brake rest puffing through dusty nostrils that are pink-edged in the sun. Johnny asks Ralph what Simon was on about at lunchtime. In the following silence I watch blue smoke drift towards silver sky. Once Ralph begins to talk he doesn't mess around.

'A bloke,' he says directly, 'got killed down Echuca and that Simon reckons some blackfella might have somethin' to do with it. Like me maybe, or another old hermit-bloke I know down there.'

'He doesn't reckon that,' I say quickly. 'He was just trying to see what you'd think of what he heard. God, it hasn't even got anything to do with you. Simon's just having you on, havin' a lend of ya.'

Johnny looks at Ralph and I. 'Why? He's not a complete drop-kick.'

'Because Ralph knew the guy who got killed,' I say, trying to sound as if I'm sick of the whole thing. Which I am. 'I think Simon thinks there might be some big story in it, so he's dangling out a hook to see what bites. You know the sort of guy he is, a TV dude.'

Ralph lifts a shoulder, scratches his chin with it. He ignores what I've said and talks to Johnny.

'I had a blue with this guy by the river, but I never hurt him bad. He turned up dead in the weir a week later, but that had nothin' to do with me.'

I swivel around to check lawyer Kate's reaction. She's watchful, her hands entwined around her knee, chin raised, eyes on Ralph.

'Are you the person Simon mentioned?' she asks. 'The one that the police want to talk to?'

'Wouldn't have a clue,' says Ralph. 'And anyway, if they wanna talk to me, here I am, eh?'

Johnny gets up stiffly, like an old dog. He sniffs, rubs a hand across his dirty old army shirt.

'Ralph, let's go check the sheep.'

Ralph gets up and without a word he and Johnny walk away into the warm insect-loaded dusk. I pull at the armhole of my singlet, feeling muscles I didn't know I had.

'Never a dull moment,' I say, putting on the cheer.

'Not when Simon's got video tape with Ralph on it,' says Kate, 'that he can send down to the Echuca cop shop whenever he likes.'

Any cheerfulness I did have leaves me. Look, eat a few too many crumpets, Kate might. Leave underwear strewn all over the countryside, she does that too – but when it comes down to straight-thinking, no one thinks straighter than Kate Hart. She's right. Ralph could be in big strife.

Diary.

*Weather: hot, again.*
*Unnamed creek.*

*We've stopped moving further away from Barramah Downs and now spend our days walking ten kilometres this way, then ten kilometres thatta-way. Even after the rain the country's as dry as it was weeks ago, if not drier. You wouldn't want to drop a match, or the whole lot'd go up. I'm sure Johnny and Kate believe Ralph's story, but I'm worried Simon might start something no one can stop. Proving you're innocent isn't always as easy as it sounds, especially when you've left town before things have been sorted out.*

*I just pray that Ralphy's not holding anything back, because if he is, the coppers'll soon figure that out. I can't help thinking about Ralph and gaol. I'm not saying he's the type to do anything suicidal – but who knows what goes through a person's mind when they're put behind bars, locked away from everything and everyone they need to keep on going?*

*Maybe, for some people, any time at all spent in prison is just too long.*

*Of course, if Ralph's innocent of any crime then he's got nothing to worry about. After all, in Australia we've got a system of justice that stretches all the way back to the days of convicts, balls and chains, floggings, and hangings. So why is it that suddenly I don't feel as confident as I did twenty seconds ago?*

# eighteen

Hot weather sweeps in from the west, the wind as dry and harsh as smoke.

'Straight off the desert,' says Johnny, as we watch the mob poking along the roadside under trees that must be sucking their water from way underground. 'Like a bloody blowtorch, burning off any grass that's left.' He rides off on Charlie, his shoulders hunched. I can feel the worry he's carrying. It's looped around him like a necklace of rusty chains. Whichever way he turns he's caught, the weight of it dragging him down.

'Hey, Johnny!' I call out to his back. 'When it rains again, it'll pour!' I hope so, God I do. I want to say more now. I want to tell him we're right behind him, that we're not just here for the cash, we're here for the meaning of the thing. To save some sheep. 'We can get through this!' I shout. 'Bloody bet on it!'

He doesn't turn, but holds a hand above his head, fingers spread, like a soldier in an old war photo I once saw; six or seven guys standing in a trench, five smoking, one holding a little dog, one waving, only two smiling. Hard to be happy when you know how serious the situation really is.

I force myself back into Bett, the towels on the seat wet but warm. Around the steering wheel I've tied strips of a dead denim shirt, the silver stud buttons pricking my hands with heat. I start Bett and mosey up towards the mob. The dogs give me a friendly look and Kate and Ralph wave tiredly. It's a long hot day all right, the third or fourth in a row, I can't remember.

I drive on through the earthy smell and noise of the sheep and keep driving. In the back I've got plastic jerrycans for water I'll have to fill from somewhere, maybe a roadside tap, an outpost pub or shop, or a farm or house. This will be our drinking and cooking water, washing water too, enough for us and maybe a shirt.

I smile as I change gear. After the Dubbo boys' second story about us went to air, people came rushing down dusty drives and across hard paddocks to give us rolls of toilet paper. I've now got about twenty. Kate and I keep the soft ones, Johnny and Ralph get the stuff you could wrap parcels in. When strangers do this kind of stuff, it does something to your heart.

One old bloke in army boots, with crooked hands, the right one missing a finger or two, waved at me with a walking stick as old as he was. When I stopped he only said one thing, but he said it twice.

'You fellas are bloody heroes,' he croaked. 'Bloody heroes! Good luck to yers!'

I don't know about that, but I have noticed that most old people and all little kids tend to say exactly what they think, which is mostly better than not saying what you think. They let you know where you stand right from the start.

'You're not too bloody bad yourself,' I yelled back. 'Take care!'

Bett and I push on, a dog in the back, a series of stark rounded hills in front. More and more the land reminds me of an ancient, giant tortoise pulling back into its hard shell. The whole country around here's going into suspended animation. In silence, in the shade and underground, living things wait for water, dead things become skeletons, the bloody cicadas sing madly. And only us and our thirsty mob push on, a live grey caterpillar inching its painful way along between the trees.

I wait at the top of the hill with a few litres of water for drovers, horses and dogs, but none for the poor old sheep.

We're passing through hill country, the track winding steadily upwards. Above us farmhouses and sheds perch, overlooking land made shadowy by the dipping sun. Suddenly, rolling down through the afternoon, through a cleft between hills, comes gunfire.

'Shooters,' I call out to Johnny who's on the flank, my stomach letting me know that the sounds are a worry. I think about those idiot spotlighters.

The boss's face is harsh, occupied by thoughts.

'Shooting, anyway.'

Shooters? Shooting? What's the diff? And then as the gunshots keep on coming I work it out. Someone is shooting sheep. Somewhere out of sight someone is working their way through a crammed stockyard with a rifle, firing, reloading, firing again. Echoes of shots and the shots themselves multiply and build. Sharp cracks and duller thwacks seem to circle overhead. I feel dizzy. Johnny shouts.

'Garn! Speak up, dogs! Hup, hup!' The boss starts to push the mob, yelling and manoeuvring on Charlie. 'Yep, go! Speak! Hup! Dirty dog! Speak up!'

Complaining loudly the sheep start to scramble, the dogs worrying them along, me driving slowly behind, breathing dust, watching for stragglers. And then we're away from the noise, slowing as Johnny holds up a hand.

'That'll do. I just couldn't bloody listen to that.'

I nod. I go on, to set up the camp. And try to put certain parts of the day out of my mind.

Diary.

14th April

*Doolittle Gorge.*
*Weather: hot.*

*My thought for the day is 'Today is history by tomorrow'. Every day we're making our own history – which makes each day seem pretty important. Like, this is your life and this is what you're doing with it. I think about Indi Em.*

*Her history and mine have become joined, like two ropes being spun into one. I still know off by heart her favourite songs and sayings. I still think of things we decided were good things. Old denim jackets for instance. Sitting on the pier. Bare feet. Tap-dancing, but never done by us! Wide straw hats. Non-hairy guys. Not-too-big waves. Pups. Volkswagens. Baths. Old bikes. Presents! There were heaps. Our futures. Twisties. Stars. Sand dunes . . .*

*As far as I'm concerned, and whether Indi knows it or not, part of my life is still hers. Perhaps the way Em and I are linked is similar to the way Ralph and the Murray River and red-gum forests at Echuca are? It's an internal thing, something that can only be really understood by those involved. These links give you strength, I reckon, fill you with a type of* love, give you ideas, and tell you in a silent way what is important and what's not.

Like, Johnny living his life by the code of the shearers' union – and Dell's memories of what she and Glen wanted to achieve. Of course, I could be wrong – but the way I feel, maybe I'm right.

Tonight the boss told this story about Jack Howe, a shearer who shore three hundred and twenty-one sheep in a day – with hand shears. He was the best, Johnny said; a wonderful shearer and a true-blue union man who supported his mates through the worst of times. In a corner of Johnny's mind, you'd be sure to find Jack Howe standing there. And when the great Jack Howe was shearing, he used to wear a type of home-made flannel singlet, and to this day in shearing sheds all over Australia, shearers still call their navy blue singlets 'Jackie Howe's'. Johnny had one on tonight, which backs up my theory. No one and nothing entirely disappears.

History is like a staircase and we're standing part way up it. Sure, you mightn't be able to see the folks right down at the bottom, but without them, how'd we get where we are now? I rest my case. And my brain for a while.

# n i n e t e e n

Another hot day, courtesy of the wicked wind from the west. And now fire. It's like we're travelling down the road to hell; the further we go the worse things get. In a paddock off to the left a grassfire stains the air with dirty blue smoke and transparent orange flames. Heat waves roll skyward, and three fat-bellied red trucks beetle around as crews in orange boilersuits and helmets lash flames with white jets of water. The firefighters seem to have the blaze cornered, but every so often a tongue of flame leaps up or fans out along the ground. I stop to watch and think, wondering if I should go back and warn Johnny. The worst thing in the world would be for the mob to be caught in a fire. That really would be hell. I don't even want to think about it.

The trucks are closer together now and I can only see small flames half the height of the grass. Steam and smoke rise angrily from the blackened earth, as if they're hissing and huffing at the hoses – but the fire's a dying dragon, almost gone. A white utility comes down the track, its windscreen fitted with a wire stone-guard dotted with dead insects. The car pulls up next to my window.

The woman driver has a tired, sun-lined face and piercing light blue eyes. She lifts a hand, then with the same hand sweeps back dark hair streaked with grey.

'You with the drovers, love?' Her voice is weary, as if she's thinking of ten things other than us and our sheep.

I tell her I am. 'Mob's about two kilometres back,' I say. 'Safe to come through, you reckon?'

The woman touches a CB radio mounted on the dashboard.

'Yeah, I was just talking to Les. He's in charge over there. They got it beat. Yeah, you can go through now, no worries.'

I look across the paddock. A train line glints in the sunlight.

'How's a fire start out there?' I ask. 'I mean, there's nothin' there to start one.'

The woman puts her ute back into first, the red knob on the column shift worn to a pale plum colour.

'Who knows? Maybe some idiot flicked a butt from the train. Maybe the sun shining through a bottle. Maybe it just started. Funny things happen. I'll see you. Be careful.'

'You, too. Thanks. 'Bye.' I watch the battered old Kingswood ute go, and I can't help but get the feeling that the whole state is fighting one big battle.

It's eerie, strange country out here. It's wide and wild, sown with boulders, the great silence like a monument to it having weathered hundreds of millions of years. The hills, the rocks and the dirt can take whatever the sun can throw down, but for the things that live there's no mercy whatsoever. Survive if you can, die if you can't. One rule for everything.

And standing by a fence, gaunt and frightening as a scarecrow come to life, is a man in patched and re-patched shirt and trousers screaming at me to, 'Get up the road, you thievin' walkabout bastards.'

I think I'd have to call that a bad omen.

On Bett's black bonnet Johnny has spread a map. He studies it intently, moving a blunt finger along the web of broken and unbroken lines that are tracks and roads. Then he folds the map and stows it back in the glove box with the roll of red tape, bandaids, ancient car service records, broken-leaded pencils, a blunt pocketknife, Lifesavers that not even I'm game enough to eat, and two heavy boxes of .22 calibre bullets. He sees me and Kate watching him as we wash vegetables in a bucket of brown water.

'Turn back for Barramah tomorrow,' he says. 'Better to be close to home if things get much worse.'

Kate and I start slowly scrubbing potatoes again, our hands moving but without any strength. We swap looks.

'How come,' she says, and drops a fleshy brown and white vegie into the bucket, 'going back should be good news, but we know it's not?'

# twenty

In desperation Johnny is taking the sheep in a straight line towards Barramah. What took us weeks to cover in zig-zags on the way out has taken us just days on the way in. The reason we are heading back? The boss reckons the better he knows the country we're travelling, the better his chance of finding water and grass. So, we'll circle Barramah Downs like a satellite, not able to touch down until the weather breaks or we have to give up. Whatever comes first.

Dunnington figures highly in Johnny's history, it being the place where his family come from – and where he thinks he ran into his grandpa's ghost. So, me being interested in the spirit-side of this world, I think I'll make a small detour into the town to see what I can see. Maybe there might be another omen around here for us? A good one. We're due for a break.

The road to Dunnington is narrow and bumpy. The fences are old, the posts grey and crooked, small farmhouses shelter behind ragged trees. I get the feeling that around here time hasn't exactly raced on by. What I'm seeing, Johnny's grandpa saw: the same wide open paddocks, the same weatherboard cottages and rounded rocks that remind me of beached whales.

Dunnington is a small place, quiet, all the houses wooden. Six shops nestle together under tin verandahs, and standing in a grassy nook is a massive and mossy old horse trough. I pull up in the shadow of the general store, park, hitch up me britches, and go in through hanging plastic streamers. Creaky floorboards announce my arrival; the cool smell of fresh vegetables is as refreshing as a wet flannel on the back of my neck. From a dark-haired lady built like an opera singer I order a milkshake.

'Drink here, lovey, or take away?'

'Here, thanks. It's nice and cool.' On the walls there are old advertising posters of Tasmanian apples, Queensland bananas, and types of ice-cream that have been extinct for years.

As the woman makes my milkshake I wander around picking up a few cans of fruit, steel wool, biscuits, and a slab of soft drinks that are on special.

'We heard you was comin',' the lady tells me quietly, putting my milkshake on the glass counter. 'Drovers. Just like when I was a kid.'

I tell her about Johnny's grandpa coming from the Dunnington hills.

'He was killed in the First World War,' I say. 'Johnny reckons there's a memorial round here somewhere.' I pay for my stuff and help load it in a cardboard box.

The shop-lady, bosoms threatening to overpower printed red roses, nods.

'Hart DR', she recites. 'KIA, France. That means Killed In Action.' She examines her hands, which are very white, then she looks at me. 'Know all the names, I do. I ought to – ' She smiles, the heaviness of her face turning into cheerful, attractive curves. 'They made us learn 'em all when we was at school. Five killed from the district, including one nurse, Sister Waldren.' Another smile, sadly this time. 'Only young fellas when they left, I guess. And still are, wherever they are. And Sister, still lovely. I seen photographs.'

I nod, slurping froth like an industrial vacuum cleaner. If I had time I'd ask my friend about spirits. She has the look of a gipsy; maybe she might be a person who knows about these things.

'I'd better scoot,' I say, and put down the grey milkshake cup. 'Could you tell – '

'I'll show you.' She comes from behind the counter and walks outside, her hair tumbling in glittering black curls. She points.

Sixty metres down the road in a small park I see a grey stone soldier standing at attention on a granite block. Behind him are tennis courts and beyond them, spreading in all directions like a carefully patched and embroidered skirt, endless paddocks.

'A nice place for it,' the woman says. 'I bet those boys'd be happy when the girls are playing tennis.' She smiles again, a careful smile that hints at certain beliefs, and wishes me luck.

I get into Bett and wave goodbye.

'Some people round here,' the woman adds, 'say that on a cold windy night – ' Again that careful smile. 'But I don't go out on cold windy nights so I wouldn't know. See you, love.'

With a slightly strange feeling niggling I drive down to the memorial and stop. The stone soldier's in full uniform, complete with a slouch hat and a rifle that I recognise as a .303, like the third-hand one my brother shoots pigs with. With ever-open eyes the Digger stares up the main street, and beyond to the biscuit brown hills and the baking blue sky. I slide out of Bett and walk around the statue's squared-off base.

In flaky gold lettering are names: Anderson WP, Baker SA, Darnly BT, Franken TL, Hart DR, Jelbart K, Kingsland NP, McKenzie RB, Morse A, Simons JO, Tregeah LF, Waldren RM (Sister). Beside five of the names is a small cross, and each of those five names has a special, sacred feel, sad and heroic. I say them to myself and feel their gentle, silent power. Every name a life, every life now just a memory.

I try to imagine the noise, the smoke, the yelling, the guns, and the fear – but I can't. Now it really is a ghosts' war, all the hatred forgotten, all the dead from all of the countries dead together. All those soldiers changed from living, hoping young blokes into faded images in unopened albums, into vague inhabitants of forgetful minds.

Seconds pass, a silent minute . . . time leaving these fellas and Sister Waldren further and further behind. I touch the stone, not a goodbye or anything – more like me reassuring them that they aren't and will not be forgotten. Any of them.

Back into Bett I climb and off I trundle, each name striking its own special and sombre note . . . Anderson . . . Baker . . . Darnley . . . Franken . . . Hart . . .

The drovers have had a hard hot day, but did manage to find the sheep water and patches of feed. Ralph quietly tells me Johnny had to shoot three ewes.

'And a lot of the others aren't looking too flash, either,' he informs me glumly. 'Hardly anything to drink's knockin' 'em rotten.' He pours water into his palm and splashes carefully up into his face. It drips off like tears.

'Every dry day brings us closer to the wet ones,' I say, then change the subject, and walk over to the fire where Johnny and Kate are helping themselves to sausages and vegetables.

'Saw your grandpa's statue,' I tell the boss as I sit and, without great enthusiasm, eat what I've cooked. 'Made a quick detour into beautiful downtown Dunnington.'

Johnny looks up, white enamel plate on his knees, sauce bottle in his right hand. A pleased look crosses his face, replacing the usual serious set of lines.

'Good on ya.'

We eat, and as usual everyone has seconds except me. I collect the dishes and drop them in the green plastic washbasin. Then I go to work with my red-handled scrubber that looks like it's been chewed by a litter of German shepherd pups.

'They were heroes, those guys,' I say, working close to the fire so I don't miss out on any conversation. I think of the names carved into the grey stone as I scrub off dried gravy and tomato sauce. 'I mean, they dropped everything, didn't they? And went all that way away for a war.' I look at Johnny who's listening to me, even if his eyes are firmly fixed on the fire. 'I mean, you only get one life, don't you? It's a lot to lose.'

Johnny gives his bung leg a helping hand to straighten it. The caliper looks as if it's forty years old. The leather's worn, the steel braces are bowed and pitted, his boot heel's worn right down on one side.

'Yeah, high stakes, all right.' He sniffs, agreeing with what he's said. 'Must've been pretty bad walkin' down the track for the last time, sayin' goodbye at the station, and wondering if you were ever going to see the old place again.'

'Imagine how they must've felt, but,' says Ralph, coming over to drop a stray dirt-covered fork into the soapy water, 'when they got home? Imagine goin' away for years, then gettin' back?' He sits on his canvas chair and sticks his boots out.

'Yep, I'd go straight down the river, throw myself in, and never leave the joint again. Ever.'

It is true that you don't really appreciate what you've got until you might lose it. And I'd say that applies to your life, your country, your friends, everything. Kate, making tea for herself and Johnny, coffee for Ralph and me, hands the boss a mug that trails a fluttering yellow tag.

'Yeah, everything seems different when you're away. Especially overseas. You miss the sky or the feeling in the air, something. That feeling of – I don't know, your own place. Your own people.'

'Yeah,' I say – not that I've ever been overseas. 'I bet a lot of those guys didn't really want to go, but they went anyway.'

'Goes to show,' says Johnny, 'you don't have to win a war single-handed to deserve a medal.'

We lapse into silence. Somehow being out here, doing what we're doing, brings the old soldiers closer. I guess that's because not much around here has changed over the last seventy-five years. Dunnington is where Johnny's grandpa lived and worked, where he left his family behind, and where he would've come back to . . . And here we are around a fire, with our horses and sheep, fighting a battle of our own.

'I can't imagine,' says Kate, pausing to blow on her tea, 'what it must be like to be asked to simply hand over your life.' I can see tiny fine blonde hairs on her upper lip – not that I'd tell her for a million bucks!

'Be bloody terrible,' says Ralph solemnly. 'Still, sometimes I guess someone's gotta fight.'

'And they never brought one of 'em home after they were killed,' adds Johnny quietly. 'Buried the boys where they fell. Wouldn't suit me. I want to be eaten by Australian worms.' He laughs, tough old buzzard that he is.

'Yeah, me too,' says Ralph, shaking his head. 'When I go, I wanna be home, not in some other joint on the other side of the world.'

'Imagine your poor old soul,' I add, 'stuck amongst a bunch of strangers who don't even speak the language.'

Kate disagrees with the tilt of her hat.

'Oh, come on. At least there's plenty of Aussies all together. And anyway, what's it really matter once you're gone? I've seen the cemeteries in France and – '

'It'd matter to me,' says Ralph. 'What about them fellas who wasn't properly found and buried? That'd matter to me and my mob a lot. Anyone'd want to be buried near home, I reckon. Blackfella or white.'

'Yeah, I guess,' says Kate. 'But a war's a war, isn't it? They're always a bloody mess.'

'True enough,' says Johnny finally. 'True enough.'

As I dry the dishes, I think of those old gold names on the memorial again, gradually flaking back into the earth. Seventy-five years on and still you can feel the power of them making their way into your memory, into the whole country I reckon, as surely as the gum trees have growth rings and the sun rises in the east.

## twenty-one

Heat. No, not forty-degree heat, but long days with no rest from the sun as it tries to bleach every touch of colour from the bush and paddocks. For the last five days Johnny's had us moving the mob up and down tracks that some of the time don't appear on any map except the one inside his head.

The air's so still you'd think a loud shout might shatter it, but when there is a noise it evaporates into thin air, leaving the cicadas to reclaim the space and redouble their efforts. Somewhere to the east is the Newell Highway, pounding with cars and trucks, but I can't see or hear it. It's like we're wandering back through time, away from civilisation to a place where water and grass are the only things worth fighting for. And fighting to find them, we are.

I mosey along in Bett on a wide but empty road, the mob a kilometre or so ahead beneath a sky pale and sick-looking with the smoke from back-burning. In the distance silvery light bursts off the windscreen of something coming this way. A truck going to a property I guess, judging by the size of the dust cloud. I drive down the hill with Tiger against my elbow, then we rattle and roll along the flats, the track ahead rising and twisting, losing itself in trees and bends.

Slowly Bett pulls herself and the horse float up the hill, me coming first to Ralphy and Rowan at the back of the mob, who are hardly pushing the ewes along as they feed on brittle grass.

'Howdy,' I say, stopping, 'you right for water?'

Ralph nods. 'Right as rain.'

We swap a dusty grin and I drive on and uphill, pushing along as slowly as an old boat, the ewes getting out of my way in their own sweet time. Towards the top of the hill I stop on a wide bend. Here I take out my U-beaut camera and snap off a few quick pictures. Looking down I get the idea the year could be 1891 just as easily as 1991. Horses, sheep – hang on, I look uphill. Forget what I just said. A big and dirty Kenworth truck with a gi-normous silver bullbar has just come into view over the top of the hill. I put Bett into first, and wait, boots on brake and clutch. What the hell's he doing here?

He'd have to be lost. And he'd better stop before he starts down this stretch, because this track's not fit for fully-loaded monsters.

He doesn't stop. Now what?

I pull on Bett's headlights, flash them, and sit with hands on the wheel, feet ready to shuffle. The truck flashes his lights. Okay, so stop, big fella. He doesn't. Instead he flashes his lights again, this time lighting up four white driving lights and two yellow fog lights. A truck horn roars.

BAAARP!

He ain't stopping. Or he can't; although by the amount of dust hurling out from underneath I think he's trying pretty hard – but getting nowhere, except closer to me. And the mob.

I rev Bett hard, drop the clutch, and swing a killer U-turn downhill. Right boot down, hand on the horn, Tiger barking, horse float swinging, I head directly for the flock and Johnny on Charlie. I change into second. Seventy, eighty metres behind, in my mirror, the truck looks to be floating on a cloud of fog and smoke, as if his brakes are locked and on fire – but still he comes, not fast, but not stopping either. And Bett's horn sounds about as effective as a bloody bicycle bell. B-e-e-e-p! B-e-e-e-p!

I close in on Johnny, waving frantically and yelling out of my window.

'Go! Get out of it! He ain't stoppin'! Go!'

Johnny rams his heels into Charlie, then charges from the fence line into the middle of the track, shouting. Sheep scatter, blundering off the road towards the fences, crashing into each other, getting caught in fallen branches, running in mobs, in pairs, the flock disintegrating like grey marbles falling out of a ripped bag.

And now I'm in amongst the ewes and still the truck's coming, its dust swallowing trees, horn blasting, speeding up on the steeper slope. Jesus! I put my foot down, then I have to hit the brakes – bloody sheep! Bang! The float butts hard at Bett from behind and the mob scatter in every direction but the right one – and now they're doubling back at me like idiotic rabbits. And still the truck's coming, huge, its orange canvas-wrapped load rising high above the red cabin.

BAAAAAARP!

I leave my hand on the horn.

B-e-e-e-e-p!

The bloody sheep aren't getting out of the road fast enough, in fact they're slow as wet weeks, but – thump! I hit one, then I hit another and another, the sensation like punches in my stomach. I yell, smack the horn, see Johnny, Ralph, Kate and the dogs, and I hear shouting, barking, sticks breaking, and hooves pounding hard dirt – but still the truck's rolling on after me, all lights lit-up, horn ploughing the air with one long deep chilling blast.

BAAAAAAAAARP!

He'll go over me, straight over me. I've got fifty metres on him but the sheep are milling and – I accelerate, Bett hauling herself and the float forwards and into noise, sheep, and dust. Sounds and smells fill the cabin, the steering wheel bucking in my hands as sheep bounce off the bullbar, flung out of the way, legs scrabbling in the air. How fast can I go? God, how fast's he going? Faster than me by the look of it.

Thump! Thump! Crunch. I hit more sheep, but I'm so worried about the horse float tipping I don't even try to miss them. I can't go too fast. Not in amongst – holy hell, here it comes.

The truck's right into the mob, amongst sheep, horses, people, dogs, and trees. I see Ralph in the middle of the road on Bruce, driving ewes into the roadside grass, then he turns downhill, racing the truck, trying to clear the way like some mad cowboy fool. And Kate's there, and Johnny, on the road, horses trampling forward, dogs racing, trying to push the mob to the fences.

Most but not all of the ewes are going. Stragglers simply disappear under the silver bullbar as if they're being sucked into a machine. Branches snap off against the truck's load and fly or hang like broken arms. And I'm hitting sheep every few metres, Bett's bullbar punching them aside, the steering wheel reefing as I run right over one, noises coming out of me that I've never heard before.

And still that bloody truck's coming, not even trying to stop now, because he's on the steepest part of the hill, and if he skids he'll go off the road, through the fence, and won't stop somersaulting for half a kilometre –

BAAAAAAAAARP!

I hit another ewe, the shock of the impact jolting up through the wheel, loosening a sob from me – but I'm almost through the flock now. Like remnants of hail after a storm there are fewer and fewer sheep and then there are none and I'm on the flat and in third gear. And still the truck's coming, bearing down, steel, chrome and wheels, smoke, thunder, and speed.

The track's level now, I'm in fourth, fear in my throat as thick as vomit. Nowhere to go but straight ahead. Trees and stumps flicker past like a broken wall and behind me the truck's bucking and swaying, burling downhill, picking up real speed. Bugger this, folks. Hang on, Tige!

Ahead on the right is a turn-off to a closed steel gate. That'll do. I steer for it, using Bett's bonnet as a sight, aiming right between the twin wooden posts, trying to brake and change down at the same time. I'm into third, slowing and bumping, I go for second, get it –

KLASHHHHHHHH!

The gate's gone, Bett's bouncing, slewing, trying to go straight ahead over turned wheels like a kid over the handle-bars of a stopped bike. I hit my head, the float leaps, tilts, tilts further, but doesn't roll. I stop, jack-knifed.

I am not moving. I am still. Bett bucks forward, and stalls. I start to cry, quickly deciding there's no good reason to stop. I can't get my breath, I can't see out of my left eye, something warm's streaming down my face and my head hurts with a deep blunt ache. Blood splashes onto my shirt, big drops splattering into little drops, all being absorbed into the soft cloth and spreading. My stomach shrinks in on itself as if I'm about to vomit – but I don't. I take a big breath.

'God, Tige,' I say, 'look at this bloody blood.' Then, instead of vomiting I faint.

There are people, but it's Ralphy I cling to. I put my arms around him and bury my face into his neck, into his smell and warmth – then he's gone and a lady is pressing something cool against my forehead and talking to me in a soft voice that washes over me like sunshine. Over and over she tells me everything is all right, all right, all right, until I begin to believe her. I force myself to stop blubbering.

I am made to sit down in the shade, away from Bett, on a blanket. Someone puts a coat around my shoulders then gives me a warm mug with Garfield the cat on it.

'It's tea, love,' my large guardian angel tells me. 'White with sugar. Drink it up, it's not too hot.'

I do what I'm told, drinking, hardly seeing or hearing, my eyes brushing over things, never stopping. There are people I don't know and cars I don't recognise. Dogs bark, someone shouts, other people whistle, a woman is feeling up and down Aileen's front legs, and there are gunshots – every so often like a handful of crackers left too close to a fire. Down the road I see a bloke sitting on the steps to the truck's high cabin, his face in his hands. I feel as if I'm going to faint again.

'Who?' I ask, then I think of something better. 'What's?' No, that's no good. 'Where?' No. 'Why?' I give up.

Again the lady in the pineapple print dress tells me everything I need to know.

'Your boss had a fall, but he's fine. Everyone's okay, the horses are all right. You lost a few sheep, that's all.' This woman's voice is like medicine or magic. I feel exactly what

163

she tells me to feel. She seems to have an investment in kindness as valuable as a vault full of gold. She tells me a doctor will be coming soon to have a look at my head.

'Only a bit of a cut,' she adds, and I believe her. She seems to know far more than I do about everything. 'Just drink your tea, dear.'

This sounds like good advice, and although I'm half-tempted to disobey, I don't. I know there are things I should ask and do, but I'll tell you, I'm just about too damn zapped to do them. Correction, I am too zapped to do them. I think I'll just sit and let the world pass on by right in front of my whacked-out eyes. And look who's coming, a man with a little black bag. Doctor Somebody, I presume.

## twenty-two

I'm in a bed, a very soft, single bed. I'm also in a room with drawn curtains fine enough to let honey-coloured light filter through. And I'm relieved to see I've got my undies and T-shirt on – but on my head I have a bump as big as the ashtrays I used to make in pottery class at school, and spiky things that I guess are stitches. What the –

I remember. God, do I. My head starts to pound and I lie right where I am, re-running memories I wish I didn't own.

What a mess. What a disaster. I hug myself and burrow deeper down into the bed. Down here I feel better, but not for long. I sit up and prop myself against a bedhead of smooth white wood. I refuse to think – about that.

On the white walls are red, yellow and blue ribbons. There must be forty of them, and a collection of silver cups, trophies and medals. I can also see framed photographs of a girl with different horses. In an effort to check things out more clearly I lean over and haul back a curtain.

Sunlight, bright and hard, shines in, showing dust specks suspended like stars. I wish I had my sunglasses. I am

165

determined not to think about – I decide I like this room with its faint smell of perfume, clothes, and the make-up of a girl who seems not to have been around for months. It's sisterly and comforting. Slowly I get out of bed and put on an old white towelling bathrobe I find behind the door. It's got a hole under one arm and pink tissues in the pocket, of which I take advantage of the cleanest two.

I blow my nose, and give up trying not to remember.

Sheer, sheer luck was all that got me through. It was luck and only luck that saved me from killing myself or someone else. Sorry, sheep. What a mess. Suddenly I know there's something I've got to do. Where's the toilet? Near the shower, I hope. Then I'll face the rest of it.

It's amazing who you find in bathrooms these days.

'Dell, what are you doing here?'

Dell, wearing neat jeans and a big white shirt, gives me a quick hug. Then she retreats to lean against the yellow basin. She looks, as usual, weary.

'Thought I'd better check you out,' she says, fiddling with a small ornamental soap shaped like a seashell. 'I heard you did something pretty wild. I'm impressed.'

I sit on the side of the bath, thoughts dashing from one side of my head to the other. There are lots of things I half remember.

'All I – ' That's as far as I get. I put my brainwaves on hold.

Dell examines the pastel-coloured soaps with distaste. Not her style, obviously. Now she crosses her arms and blows a strand of hair away from her face.

'Considering what might've happened,' she says, 'I'd say you're all lucky to be alive. Here, I brought you a toothbrush.'

She takes out three new toothbrushes from her jeans pocket.

'Red, green, or white?'

'Eeny meeny miny mo, catch – '

'Take one, Lal.'

I take one, thank her for it, and ask how the rest of the crew are, dogs, horses, and sheep included.

I sit at a yellow laminex kitchen table with Dell and Iris, the lady who calmed me down with kindness and tea after the massacre. She and her husband Jack were the first on the scene after I'd completed my illegal right-hand turn through the shut gate. I am given another cup of tea and asked what I'd like for breakfast.

I think I'm in heaven. I request a boiled egg and toast fingers, and tell Iris as she rambles around the non-renovated kitchen that I like the room I slept in. She sets the egg-timer going, sits next to Dell, and pats me on the hand with strong warm fingers.

'That's Jacinta's room. She's at boarding school. And she's horse-mad, if you couldn't tell.'

Suddenly a sizeable chunk of guilt dongs me on the head.

'Was that your gate I went through? Look, I – '

Iris laughs, putting a hand to her chest, where a pair of Dame Edna-style reading glasses hang on a clear plastic chain.

'The gate! Oh beggar the gate, dear. Jack can fix that.'

I slowly finish my egg and tea then stand. I ask where the rest of the crew is.

'I guess I'd better go see them,' I say. 'They can't do a thing without me.'

I walk unsteadily up the track to the old white fibro cement shearers' cottage and force open a rusty gate. Someone has even tried to make a bit of a garden here. Iris, I bet. Three giant daisy bushes, gone feral, hold on tight to the hard brown soil. I step up onto the porch and peer through a torn screen door into a dark front room. Swags and clothes are heaped on the floor.

'Hey, Ralphy,' I call out, 'what d'you think this is? Bush week?'

There's the sound of chairs scraping. From somewhere, maybe the kitchen, Kate and Ralph appear, looking clean, combed and well-fed. We exchange big silly smiles, I drag open the door and on the verandah we hug. I could burst into tears if I let myself.

'You're a hero, Lal,' says Ralph. 'If you hadn't come down the track in old Bett we would've copped it something shockin'.'

I don't know where to look or what to do with my hands. I give Ralphy a light whack.

'You guys didn't do too bad yourselves. I saw you in action.' A flash of memory hits me: Ralph, Kate and Johnny on the horses, with dogs and the mob and the rolling red truck – I look at Kate. Her hair's pulled back and shines like polished pine. Her ears are pierced with tiny gold studs. 'You guys can really ride,' I say. 'I've never seen anything like it. Where's Johnny-boy?'

Ralph dumps himself down in an old green chair by the door. He gazes out at paddocks, fences and a hayshed lumpily carpeted with just a few yellow bales.

'He's gone with Jack to check the sheep.' He looks at me briefly, then back out to the sun-drenched paddocks. 'To see if they can keep going or whether they've had it.'

Diary.

26th April

'Gurrawang' 25 km south of Barramah Downs.
Weather: hot and humid.

*We're staying at Gurrawang with Jack and Iris Bolton for another night. Later this afternoon a vet's coming to have a proper look at the sheep. If he says they can't go on, we'll shoot them here tomorrow. No point pushing them all the way back to Barramah to die there. In a shed Jack's got a bulldozer which he said he'd drive for us, if we need a huge pit.*

*I'm writing this quickly because if I think about it too hard I'll be a blubbering mess.*

*Just before lunch Johnny took us all aside and told us he'd never forget what we did, which only makes it worse to think we might lose the old girls now. It'd be heartbreaking, and just about send Johnny to the brink, I reckon. But Bush Rules still rule: if the mob can't walk, the mob can't live. Looks like the TV boys might miss out on the third part of their story, unless pictures of a big hole in the ground are any good to anyone.*

Outside I can hear something rumbling. Maybe it's thunder or maybe it's Jack starting up the bulldozer, I don't know, but I'm going to find out. Either we've struck it lucky – or we've struck right out.

# twenty-three

The first thing I see when I go outside is the flicker of distant lightning. I feel as if it's struck me. A blast of hot wild hope shoots from my feet to the tips of my fingers. Instantly I'm tingling and shouting and running. I run up past the dusty cars and the machine shed to the shearing quarters, only to meet Ralph and Kate coming the other way.

'It's comin' from the west,' says Ralph, his shirt wide open to show a stomach lightly ridged with muscle. 'Hope it's got some juice left in it for us.'

'Say that again,' says Kate, her eyes pink-rimmed. Dust mites in the cottage, she reckons, although I didn't see any myself. She sips from a can of lemon mineral water, then offers it.

I take it, feeling the slippery coldness of its sides, and when I tilt it to drink, instead of white sun all I can see is grey. And when I hand it back I see there's not a shadow to be seen for miles. The sun's gone into hiding. Hallelujah.

'Geez, it looks all right,' I say.

We walk down between an old wooden shearing shed and a tin building that contains huge oat bins. The air is warm but feels thick, as if it stands in one huge humid block. My skin feels thick and clammy and my underarms are damp and prickly, but I'm prepared to put up with that in exchange for any gift of rain at all.

The three of us climb onto a loading bay at the back of the shearing shed to watch the storm roll towards us, and hopefully right over us. The cloud looks like a huge piece of black land being towed. It shudders with lightning, lit up by mauve flashes as sudden as explosions, and when the thunder comes it comes as if from kilometres underground, creaking and cracking, rolling, growling, and grumbling, but never booming. The air is tight, pressurised, and the tin roof of the woolshed ticks like a time bomb. It has to rain.

'There's Johnny, Jack and the vet.' Kate points down the slight slope to three distant figures walking around our sheep. 'Surely if it's going to pour they wouldn't shoot them, would they?' She leans tiredly back against wood that is cracked and blackened with age. 'They've been travelling okay, haven't they? They've been doing all right.'

She rubs her temple as if she's got a headache.

For a while no one says anything. We know for the last three days the ewes haven't been travelling very well at all.

'Yeah,' says Ralph, 'they've been doin' okay. Bit of rain'll spark 'em up.' He studies the paddocks that look as hard and dry as bark. 'Spark everything up, bloody me included.'

Johnny, Jack, and the vet come up through a gate. They walk slowly, heads down, like three policemen discussing a murder. When Jack looks up I wave. They alter their direction and come through a gate between the oat bins and the shed. We drop down from the platform.

'Gonna rain,' I say, and tilt my head towards the cloud that's now like a black iceberg closing in. 'You can smell it.' You can, a delicate, sweet smell, with overtones of dust and mystery.

'Better than that,' says Jack, securing the rusty gate with a rusty chain, 'you can see it.' He points with a heavy-boned arm, his elbow bent like a wrinkled hinge.

He's right. In places you can see the cloud being torn down and actually sweeping the ground like mighty horse tails. It's pouring there. Has to be. But that hasn't answered our question about the sheep.

'How are the sheep?' No point holding back.

'The sheep can go on,' Johnny says tautly. 'Alex here – ' He introduces us to the vet, a guy about his own age so neat and clean he might've stepped from the window of a Fletcher Jones store. We shake Alex's freckled, pale hand.

'Alex here's gonna fix it with the shire so that we won't have to do the normal ten kilometres a day until we get home. With good water, touch wood, and a couple of decent feeds of oats in 'em we'll make it.' The boss looks at the sky that has been so hard on us.

And still we haven't been hit by a drop.

Johnny, Jack and Alex walk off up past the old shed whilst us three climb back up on to the platform to wait for the rain. I would've liked to say something to Johnny, but in front of everyone it might've backfired. In this line of work, sometimes the best way to support your mates is to shut up, sit down, wait and see.

Bingo. A raindrop as fat as a tadpole splats on my cheek. And another and another and now they're hitting the wool-shed roof, sounding like rifle slugs bouncing around a shooting gallery. Music to the ears! Medicine for the soul! Rain.

I move from the house to the shearers' quarters to be with the others. I sling my swag onto an old striped mattress and go back out onto the verandah where Kate and Ralph are sitting, bare feet on the rail, drinking stubbies in yellow foam coolers.

'Here,' says Ralphy, reaching down beside his chair. 'Gotcha a coldy. No holder, but.'

I take the beer. 'No bloody chair, either, but ta anyway.' I sit, leaning against the wall, drinking and watching the rain. It comes straight down, drilling into the bare ground. 'Direct from heaven,' I say. 'Di-rect.'

'Beer or the rain?' Ralph eyes me across the top of the small brown bottle.

'Both.'

We sit, letting the sound of rain on the corrugated roof lull us. Water spills down a pipe and gurgles merrily into a galvanised tank. The sky seems close and all there is to be heard is liquid softly hitting things. Barramah Downs included, I hope.

'Johnny's still lookin' down the barrel,' says Ralph suddenly, 'ain't he? Like this rain's gotta keep up, he's gotta feed the mob when he gets 'em home, wool prices have gotta – '

'Change the subject, sport,' I say, watching drips run along the bottom of rusty guttering. 'This is a real good start.'

'Yeah, one thing at a time,' says Kate. 'So, when all this is finished, Lal, the droving – what do you think you might do?'

I put down my empty stubby. Already I can feel the effect of it right behind my eyeballs. What am I going to do? Well, what am I going to do?

'Stuffed if I know,' I say. 'Write a book on my experiences with you two wombats, I guess.'

I don't think so! I pick up a square of tinfoil that used to be wrapped around a lolly, and fold it.

'No, maybe I'll have a holiday. Go to the snow.' Hell, where'd that idea come from? 'I dunno,' I add. 'What are we gonna do, Ralph?'

Ralph pushes his chair back so the two front legs are off the ground.

'Like to get home pretty soon. Gettin' homesick, eh?' He twists around to look at me, a light sheen of sweat on his forehead. 'Lookin' forward to seeing everybody. I'll take you out on the river, catch some crays, couple of bloody carp.'

Sounds good to me. I'd love to go down to the Murray, see the forest, meet Ralph's family, go out on the water, maybe even have a talk to the Riverman himself.

'Any jobs down there?' Kate nurses her stubby, the yellow foam bright against khaki shorts. She sips it, giving Ralph time to think before answering.

His answer's even worse than mine – and I'm using the excuse I've got concussion.

'Wouldn't have a clue.' Ralphy won't look at Kate; he looks out at the land where barbed wire runs off towards trees smoky in the distance. 'I'll find something, if I go, that is. Pickin' fruit maybe.'

Kate nods sombrely, taking in the sadness in Ralph's voice.

'What about you, Kate?' I ask, tit-for-tat. 'You made up your mind yet? About uni?'

A single line divides her forehead. Obviously she's been thinking about this; and like Ralph and I, she doesn't seem to have an answer. Or a good answer, anyway.

'I don't know. Sometimes law seems – ' She picks at the white-and-red stubby label, rolling the damp scraps between her fingers, tossing them out into a puddle blistered with drops. '– like a good thing to do, other times I think it'd be better to hand out soup to the old blokes who sleep under bushes. At least you can see that's worthwhile.'

Ralph brings his chair back down onto the verandah, ejects forward, and stands looking out at the rain.

174

'I'm gonna go check on the horses and dogs.'

Kate and I watch him walk down the small boot-beaten path. Suddenly, maybe sensing our eyes on his back, he turns like a dancer, jumping and spinning, landing to crouch down low, hands on dirt, a smile splitting his face.

'Things'll be okay!' he yells, showing us muddy palms. 'It's rainin'!' He turns and jogs off, a hundred dark spots on the back of his faded black T-shirt.

Kate and I sit, she as usual looking calm, me as usual feeling and looking a little peaky. My head pounds a bit. I guess I shouldn't be drinking. Kate finishes her beer and puts the stubby holder down.

'Drover one day, lawyer the next,' she says. 'Doesn't sound possible, does it?'

It does, with her. I hand her back an earring that's fallen into a fold of her shirt.

'You'd do it on your ear,' I tell her, 'pardon the pun.' I stand up slowly. My head stays on. 'Let's get dressed up for tea. You've got a nice clean shirt I can borrow.'

# twenty-four

We leave Gurrawang and the beautiful Iris and the wonderful Jack Bolton behind. In a hole in their bottom paddock are fifty-three of our sheep, but things could've been far worse. Between a runaway truck and thirst, heat and hunger, our droving days could've been all over, like yesterday. But they're not. We go on.

In the float is Aileen, a horse that doesn't seem to be able to bear a grudge. I thought she mightn't be too pleased with me after her last roller-coaster ride at my hands, but she's either forgiven or forgotten, bruised legs, chest and all. She walked straight up the ramp like a big friendly dog, and now her long grey face, with white forelock, can clearly be seen watching my every move.

I must admit my hands and feet were shaky when I first got back into Bett, but now, going slowly through wet countryside I feel fine. I should've known the old girl'd never let me down, and neither would any of my other droving mates. Gently I drive on, having given the flock a good head start because I wanted to have a final cup of tea with the Boltons and hear the weather forecast.

By the way, there's a storm warning out for all of north-eastern New South Wales, which I find hard to believe – because the rain's already here, isn't it?

With Jeannie, a peanut-butter sandwich and a stick, I leave the camp to walk back to the sheep. The paddocks smell divine, a cross between wet hay, leaves, and the indefinable magic mist of clouds. I spot Ralphy in front of the mob, riding along on little Brucie, the two of them looking to have all the time in the world. I squat and wait with Jeannie, who's staring lovingly at what's left of my sandwich. I give it to her, breaking all rules about how to treat a sheepdog.

'Don't tell anyone I did that,' I tell her.

She eats the crust, looking decidedly disappointed by it. I can understand that. I stand and move out onto the puddly road.

'Hey man, how's it going?' Good, it seems. He raises his hat.

Ralph always looks totally relaxed riding. His wrists, elbows, shoulders and hands are loose, but never too loose.

'Howdy.' He slouches forward in the saddle, like cowboys do when they're rolling themselves a smoke. Poseur! 'Brake up all right, is it?' he asks.

'Nah, I burnt it on the fire.' I walk beside the horse, having to pick my pace up a bit to do so.

'Been a few patches of feed,' says Ralph. 'Least there's plenty of water around.'

We walk, the sheep behind us not making as much noise as when the going's dry and everything crackles and snaps. It's so good to feel cool and clean for a change. Everyone's mood has lifted; the future's not rushing at us like a fire or a dust storm.

'Been good this droving, ain't it?' says Ralph suddenly. 'I'm glad we came, eh? Good to get outta the tent. I might've been carried out if it wasn't for you, Lal.'

'You'd have done the same for me. Forget it.' He would've, I know it. 'But you've got to admit it was pretty interesting back there for a while. With Barley.' I shape up, like an old-time lord of the ring, then let my hands drop. 'Looking back that is.'

It seems a long time ago. And like a film, larger than life, with amazing characters living amazing lives. And we were there, amongst it: the fighters and the fights, the towns, pubs, country racetracks, caravan parks and the endless driving. And now we're here, and it has been good this droving, maybe brilliant – but I won't know that until we've finished, and my memories have sorted themselves out like sifted sand and pebbles. Ralph swings around to check on the mob. I see Kate on the fence line on Massy. She waves, hanky fluttering. I wave back, bumping my elbow on Ralph's stirrup.

'Steady,' he says, 'I gotta get a few more days outta that boot.' He lifts a handful of reins towards his shoulder. 'She turned out all right, Kate, didn't she? At the start I thought she mightn't like us much.'

'You're not wrong,' I say, then tap my chest with a fist. 'Her heart's in the right place, even if the rest of her comes from Sydney, eh?'

'She's got heaps goin' for her,' Ralph says steadily. 'There's not many people you can really like after working right next to 'em, but she's one, I reckon. She's got guts and you can trust her.'

Without warning a barbed feeling skewers my throat. I look at Ralph's face, at his shoulders that are as elegant and supple as the wings of a hawk, at his long loose back, and suddenly I think he and I are moving apart. Something between us is changing, but I don't know what. Ralphy suddenly seems older and wiser and I just seem to be the same silly old Lal.

Sadness floods me. I don't want Ralphy and me to split up — even though we're not even officially together. Best friends are hard to find, and I should know, having already lost the only other one I've ever had. Here and now, I know, isn't the right place to say what I'm going to say, but I'm going to say it anyway. Timing's never been one of my strong points.

'Ralphy,' I say. 'Stop for a minute.'

Ralph stops Bruce, and perhaps seeing something in my face, he slides down to the ground.

'What, you wanna ride?' He grins, offers me the reins that are the same colour as his hands.

I shove them away. 'No, I just want to say that you're my best friend, you dope.' Words come speeding out as I look up at him. 'I just want you to know that in case I don't get time to say it later. I love you, Ralph, and I always will, whatever happens.' I push a finger into his chest. 'You and Indi Em. My best friends, ever.' There. Said it. Everything.

See? Heart on sleeve. Who cares?

Ralph turns away, looking off at the trees whose leaves are now thick, moist and clean. My face is burning, but that doesn't matter. Ralph puts out a hand, moves it inside my shirt and onto my shoulder. It's warm, wide, and firm.

'You, too, Lal. My best friend.' His face has a concerned look, as if we mightn't be speaking the same language. 'I mean, what I said about Kate before, I like her, but that's all. I'm not like –'

Suddenly sheep surround us, streaming past, skittering away, making a racket, added to by Jeannie who's rushing at them, nipping and darting, prodding at fleecy legs with her sharp brown snout. Ralphy laughs, then mounts up and trots forwards.

'Catch you later, Lal. Come 'ere, dogs! Come 'ere to me now!' Ralph's voice is merry. He swivels around. 'Bad news when you get passed by a bunch of bloody old sheep!' He rides off, me watching him, hoping he'll turn around again, but he doesn't.

I walk on, trying to think of all the different types of love there is. Okay, there's love for brothers, sisters and parents, love for friends, love for best friends, love for dogs, love for cockatoos which is different from love for dogs, love for triers – and then there's the big one – the special hearts-and-arrows type of love you carve in a tree for all to see.

So, which type of love are Ralph and I talking about? Best friends, yes, but best friends only? I mean, surely love's the slipperiest kind of thing to try and put or keep in just the one category? Of course it is. It's impossible to pin down, because if you do try to pin it down, it might just puncture like a balloon.

I walk on with sheep that don't seem keen on keeping me company. They run off in dithery groups, flicking their ears and showing me their bums. Charming. By the way, where does lust, and love for chocolate come into what I was saying before? Somewhere. I dunno, but I do know I'm too weary to think about it.

*Diary.*

*1st May*

*Somewhere between Gurrawang and Barramah Downs.*
*Weather: warm, breezy, cloudy.*

*The sheep travelled all right today, although we only did six kilometres. I'm sure they'll all make it back to Barramah, but as to what happens over the next few weeks or months I wouldn't want to guess. It takes a lot of rain to drown a drought.*

*Today's been interesting. I guess when you're as close to someone as I am to Ralph you don't notice them changing, you can only gradually realise that they have. Ralph seems stronger than he was, and I'm sure he's a better judge of people. This is good, of course, but I only hope that I'm not going to lose a friend as if I was a sailor fallen overboard, and he's a ship that'll go chugging on into the night. Wrong. Ralph hasn't abandoned me. No way – but if he has choices to make, or a new direction to go in, then I'll wish him the best of luck with all my heart . . . because you can't stop a person changing. Maybe we both have? Maybe our friendship will simply get stronger? Bring us closer together, who knows? What I do know is . . . that something strange has just happened. The wind has died away.*

*It's as if the world has stopped. I'm listening hard, although there's nothing to listen to. I hold my breath as if something's about to happen, but nothing does. It is just so still. Enough of the diary, I'm going back to the fire. It wasn't spooky over here before, but it is now.*

Johnny, Kate and Ralph stand in the dark around the fire, their empty chairs behind them. I seem to make a huge racket just walking through the grass.

'God, it's quiet, isn't it?' I say, joining the circle, automatically putting my hands out to the flames.

'Stars are still there,' says Kate. 'It's weird. So still. I don't like it. It's creepy.'

Ralph moves his feet uneasily. 'Storm comin', Johnny? Maybe we better tie things down a bit? Extra rope around the horses and sheep.'

Johnny smells the air, pulls a face, drops a hand onto his leg with a slap.

'Hard to tell. Can't see anything, can I? Can't hear anything, either. What are the dogs doing?'

The dogs are standing still, except for Jeannie who's walking around uneasily, taking small delicate steps, sniffing the air, wagging her tail slowly when she sees us looking at her.

'Better be safe than sorry,' says the boss, and backs away from the fire, his bung leg stiff like a prop. 'Ralph, rig a tarp from the truck for the swags, Kate, let the horses out into the paddock – there's a gate behind us – and Lal, stow the boxes and do whatever. I'll go strengthen up the brake a bit.'

We scatter, me able to hear clearly the sounds of what all the others are up to as I work, then work faster as I hear a low roaring that could be a tidal wave, but must be wind sweeping towards us.

'It's on its way!' yells Johnny, his voice hammering back through the trees. 'Once you've done what you're doin', get back to Bett. If there's gonna be lightning that's the safest place. Lal, chuck water on the fire!'

I sling the last of the swags under Ralph's half-completed tarp, grab a bucket, and head for the fire. The roaring is getting louder. It's right behind me and the hairs on the back of my neck are sticking up. At any moment I expect to be flattened, by what I don't know, but the sound of it's wide and low, as if a goods train is coming, charging out of the dark, flat-out.

Without warning, sparks are ripped from the fire and strewn into the bush. I up-end the bucket, sending steam chasing off after them. The wind is hard and cold and getting harder, colder and stronger by the second. It smells too, of rain. Trees bend, bow and shake, canvas chairs flip and roll, empty buckets bounce, and sticks and leaves sweep down like sharp hail. Kate I see struggling with the horses, so off I go, through the beating bush, and grab Charlie by the bridle.

'Through the gate!' Kate shouts, her voice riding away on the wind. 'Then let him go!'

I run, trying to see what's on the ground, trying to drag Charlie along as he tosses his head, snorts and tries to go sideways. Fifty metres seems like five hundred. The gate's open, I take the horse into the paddock, let the halter go and watch as he canters off into the roaring blackness, mane and tail whipping. Kate brings in a flighty, prancing Massy and does the same.

'That's it!' she yells. 'Quick, out, the other two are in, I'll shut the gate.' She runs to it, and I run past, pushed sideways by the wind, then we're in the bush.

Above our heads the trees whip and whiplash, branches crack and collapse, the noise of flogging leaves coming in rolling waves. We make it back to Bett, tear open a door, and pile in like frightened mice. I see Ralph run out of the darkness, hand on his hat, keeping low as if he was dodging bullets. He fights the wind for control of a door, wins, and gets in.

'Geez, bloody strong!' He has to yell. 'Don't know how long that tarp'll last! Unreal, ain't it!'

I can hear the tarp slapping like a shaken mat, I can see trees thrashing, I can feel the storm running over us like an angry sea. Bett's rocking like a boat, and suddenly lightning sizzles, the camp and bush immediately lit up neon-blue and black.

'Shit, wait for it!' Ralph's voice is clear in the split second of silence.

We hunch down into each other's shoulders and Bett's comforting old seat.

KABOOOOOOM!

The thunder knocks us sideways. It hits once like a hammer, then seems to split to the east and the west, then crashes in on us again from both directions, rolling and trampling, seeking us out with sounds so loud they erupt in mid-air rather than arrive.

Johnny turns up, hatless, his shirt wind-wrapped to his ribs as he opens the passenger-side door. We squash up in the cabin that's now hot, damp and cramped. A window winder sticks into my leg like a blunt spear.

'Bloody hell!' the boss says, gasping. 'She's wild. I'm gonna go back to the brake. I didn't think it'd get like this.'

There's a new sound now. A beating drumming sound, brought to us on the wind, and now it's raining, bucketing, absolutely pouring. The invisible sky is a waterfall. Rain is being driven so hard it sounds like a rock slide on Bett's unyielding roof and bonnet. She'll cop a few scars out of this, for sure. Lightning flashes blue, blackness bounces back, thunder cracks and shakes, the rain pounds down. Johnny laughs.

'Stuff the drought!'

I suddenly realise that I'm enjoying myself here in Bett. It's good, everyone in together; reminds me of cubbyhouse days with Em and the crazy Trevaskis twins, Gonzalo and Thor. I feel safe as houses, even though I know we're not. A tree could wipe us out, or by the look of the rain, we could drown. If Bett was a boat before, she's a submarine now. All I can see and hear is water and more water.

'What d'you reckon the sheep'll make of this?' I yell, looking out at the flashing landscape through a windscreen that gives the impression that we're fish in a bowl.

'Better find out,' says Johnny. 'Carn Ralph. Got yer togs?'

'Yep.' And the two of them bale out, a cold blast of rain and wind roaring in to take their places.

I look at Kate, she looks at me. As nice and safe as it is in the ute . . .

'Let's go!'

We scramble out into the wind and water, mud underfoot, leaves flying overhead, trees moaning. We dash after Ralph and Johnny and I'm laughing, a mix of hysteria and joy, amazed at what I'm doing, happy that Kate's with me, two mad sheilas on a mad mission. I stumble, Kate drags me roughly up, and on we go, dwarf figures struggling on through an inland rainforest. Or it is at the moment.

Thirty metres to the left a tree crashes down, and as if this was the starter's flag, hail begins to fall in sheets. Billions of iceballs whack, smack, rattle and bounce. Now the air is blue with lightning, streaked with ice, and the ground is rolling and flowing in all directions. Again lightning cracks the sky and thunder threatens to split the ground.

KABOOOOM BOOM BOOM BOOM!

The loudness stops us dead, but the brake's ahead, and I can make out Johnny and Ralph circling it. On we go, forcing through sodden bracken, sticks tearing, grass snagging.

'We're here!' I yell, and grab a stake that's leaning inward and hold onto it for dear life.

The sheep are bunched, a pale moving mass in the dark, noisy as ever, but not panicking yet. I kneel, not wanting to scare them any more than they already are, and feel a flurry of pain across my back as the hail hits.

I crouch, head and shoulders twisted, hands gripping the stake, my knuckles smacked by ice – but I do not let go. I grip that stake. And Kate I see is doing the same, kneeling, holding on, our only job to keep the brake upright.

For once in my life I know exactly what I have to do, what I should do, what I want to do, and what I will do. I'll hold on. I laugh into my chest. I don't think holding a stake requires much talent, but it occurs to me suddenly that some of the most important things I ever do don't require too many brains or too much training – they just require basic willpower. Which I seem to have, and so does Kate. So hold on we will. Unless one of us gets struck by lightning.

# twenty-five

Early morning shows us a camp that looks like it's been done over by a heavyweight wrecking crew. Just about everything that could've blown over, fallen over, collapsed, or broken, has. And speaking of crews, look out – because here's another one. The white DTV 5 Commodore is back.

Or at least Sly Simon is.

He parks the station-wagon behind Bett, gets out, lights a cigarette and walks over to the fire, his white polo shirt bright against a background of wet dirt, wet bark, sodden clothes, a carpet of leaves and sticks, and us – looking like refugees from a bombed barge. Slimy Simon seems to be trying not to smile, but he can't stop it. It takes over his face despite him trying to get rid of it by slowly shaking his head. That doesn't work, so he scratches a furrow through his blond hair and takes a good look around.

'Well,' he says slowly, 'this is certainly another fine mess you've got us into, Ollie.'

There's silence, then Ralph laughs, then Johnny, then me. Only Kate's unamused.

'What d'you want, waste of space?' She stands there in a pair of baggy blue shorts wet on the bottom. 'Where's your camera and your goofy mates?'

Simon indicates the car with a twisted thumb.

'Camera's in the car. I'll get a few shots in a minute. Boys are back at Barramah setting up a bit of stuff with Dell. How about a coffee? I've been lookin' for you guys for hours.' He kneels down, tosses a couple of wet sticks on the fire, then wipes black scraps of bark off his hands. He looks up, his face so smooth I wonder if he ever has to shave. 'So, when'll you hit Barramah? I've been sent to find out.'

'Two days,' says Johnny. 'On the nose. Unless there's another cyclone we don't know about.'

Ralph tosses Simon a clean mug.

'Have milk do ya, mate?'

'Nah,' says Simon. 'Black, thanks sport. So how've things been, Ralph? All quiet on the western front?'

I walk away before I say something I might live to regret.

We move on through a tattered landscape. The roads are covered with storm litter, creeks are running, dams are filling, clouds catch up to us then roll on by. I can hear frogs! I also manage, on a greasy uphill elbow corner, to bog Bett, but with eight tonnes of wood, twenty minutes of digging and some luck, I get out and go slewing on off up the track, feeling like an ironwoman and a pioneer. A muddy ironwoman and pioneer.

We're heading straight for Barramah, all systems go. The mob, filled to the brim with water, are doing close to the usual ten kilometres a day. As Johnny said, we'll hit the front gate tomorrow arvo and hope that somehow there's enough grass for the sheep to eat until the new stuff grows.

Friends and neighbours of Johnny and Dell come out to visit, some tooling along on ag. bikes or on horses they've floated out for the day. People I've never met before roll up and say gidday. Women hug me, hand over nice things to eat wrapped in greaseproof paper. Big blokes shake my hand, kids ask mad questions, two handsome young dudes in white hats kiss me. And one big burly guy sticks his head into Bett, bringing a bottle's worth of Brut aftershave and a gust of beery breath.

'Howdy, Spike,' he says, huffing and puffing as he jogs alongside, 'long time no see. Hey, your hair's grown! You actually look like a sheila.'

I remember this dude. I tug his hat forward, put my foot down, and leave him standing. I wave out the window. He yells after me.

'Ya look better on TV than ya do in real life, Spike!'

I give him the finger, light-heartedly of course, and drive on, just the teeniest weeniest bit hacked off that Dell hasn't bothered to come out and see us. Maybe things are worse back at Barramah than anybody's letting on?

Lighting the fire for the last night is like giving the trip its last rites – but instead of us going out in a puff of smoke I drag in heaps of wood and build up a roaring blaze. The smell of flaring gumleaves is sweeter than incense, the sound of crackling sticks is like listening to a favourite story. I look around me. Everybody's working, taking care of sheep or horses or dogs or saddles. So this is it, folks. The last night of being with my fire, my pots, my pans, my buckets, my billies, my boxes, my axe, my swag, my truck, my job . . . my dogs, my horses, my sheep, my friends, my sky, my stars, my trees, my land.

I never realised I had so much.

# twenty-six

We strike camp and move out, our sheep show on the road for the last time. I drive off, the colours of the country pressing themselves at me, the bumps of the road hinting at adventures to be had, if only I'd keep on driving, driving, driving. And our sheep walk onwards, a big bleating mob keen on hanging in there.

Today I'll stay close to them, just ambling along in Bett, stopping to boil a billy for the crew or just to look at paddocks. No way do I want to turn up at Barramah Downs by myself. No thanks. If there's going to be a welcome home party I want to rock along with my friends, all nineteen hundred and forty of them.

It's a funny thing, but I feel quite lonely. I feel like I feel when a holiday's just about over and all that's left to do is pack up, go for a last walk, then drive home. A part of my life has passed. Not much can happen now, I don't think, but as Johnny says, 'it ain't over until it's over' and perhaps he has a point – I just saw a black cat splattered on the road.

We insist Johnny leads the sheep in over the last kilometre. So he rides to the head of the mob, Tiger trotting in the shadow of Charlie-horse, and takes the ewes in off the dirt, onto the bitumen, and through his front gate – under a banner strung between a couple of old goalposts.

WELCOME HOME it says in blue lettering on white sheets, and welcome home we feel.

There's a noisy crowd on the weedy lawn in front of the little crooked white house, a couple of trestle tables set up with a silver beer barrel below, and plenty of clapping and shouting going on. But it's the Dubbo television guys who escort us in, walking backwards up the track, Simon's black-eyed camera on Johnny, Knobs pointing his mike, and Jeff walking alongside Charlie-horse, lobbing questions up at the boss.

Suddenly tears threaten to overwhelm me. I know these bush people are not my people and I know that this place is not my home – but I'm being treated as if it is. Surely if Barramah Downs' paddocks are as full of goodness as the folks around here, then the grass has to grow. That's not too much to ask, is it? Surely.

*Diary.*

*6th May*

*Barramah Downs.*
*Weather: cool and clear.*

*I'm writing this sitting on a bed, which I'm very much looking forward to getting into. We've just had a big Dell-cooked dinner, the Dubbo boys included, and for once no one had to go and check on the sheep. Yes, the droving's over. And for every kilometre travelled, and there were about five* hundred, I reckon we got to know each other almost as well as we got to know ourselves. Your true colours will always show through dirt, no matter how thick it is.

I didn't occur to me until now that Johnny Hart was actually pretty patient with Ralph and me. He took a risk hiring us, and he watched us like a cop, and he told us off a lot, but he made sure we learnt to do what we had to do. Okay, those skills weren't mind-bogglingly difficult to learn, but you stuff up, and it could've been . . . Maybe what we did learn was to stick to our guns.

And Ralphy, away from the boxing tent, his gentleness and concern just grew until it included all sheep, horses, dogs and drovers. He was watching out for everyone. I reckon he'd make a great nurse and I'm not joking. I'll tell him that one day, too. Not many people care about every living thing on the planet like Ralph does.

Tomorrow we move on, with cheques and references, although what the next step for me and Ralph is I don't know. Yep, it's all over, Red Rover. Or just about.

For some reason Jeff, Simon and Knobs are hanging around until tomorrow. There's obviously something happening, but every time I ask the boys they shrug and wander off, leaving behind some pathetic excuse. Wait and see I guess. Why not? I'm in no hurry to go anywhere.

## twenty-seven

After breakfast I'm sitting outside drinking coffee, watching the Dubbo boys mucking around with their gear. I see Jeff walk off around the house, a mobile phone stuck to his ear, Simon following him, tapping at his diver's watch, obviously concerned about one thing or another. Something's brewing, and unless it's tea, I'm not sure if I like it.

Ralph comes outside and sits next to me, not saying a word. He looks well-scrubbed, his shirt and jeans ironed, his boots polished. His hair, pulled back into a flaring ponytail, some-how smells of apples. His sleeves are rolled, his hands are still, he looks across the paddocks to the south where gum trees spread up and back into hills, blue-green with distance.

'Johnny's gonna teach me to shear,' he says suddenly. 'I'll be staying here for a while, Lal.' He breathes in deeply through his nose and lets out a breath. 'If things work out. I'm sorry I, I only just found out. He only just asked me.'

The words stop my thoughts and my breath. I actually have to order myself to fill my lungs, and when I do they hurt. I feel like I've hit a wall. Thump. Bang. Wallop. I've been flattened, and all I can see from where I am is the future rearing up like a big dark cloud. I'm alone again, just like that.

Ralph is looking at me, I'm looking at nothing.

'I'm sorry, Lal.' His voice is as soft as the fingertips he's touching my wrist with. 'I had to say yeah, didn't I? I mean, I'll be workin' for nothing, just the shearing. It's me only chance, Lal. You understand?'

Ralph's head is close to mine. I look at the complicated curling of his ear. So that's how we hear words, is it? So that's how we learn what I know is the truth of the matter. Of course Ralph's got to take this chance, and of course Johnny can't keep me on. Hell, this ain't no charity. I'll survive. I always have, haven't I?

Of course I will. I'm not even angry. I'm not. Sad yes, lonely for sure, desolate absolutely, and hurt a . . . bit, but angry? No. This is an opportunity for Ralph, and a bloody good one. At least one of us has taken a step in the right direction.

'I'm not angry, Ralph,' I say slowly, 'I'm rapt, just that it's taking me a while to get used to the idea.' I pick a piece of grass and run it between my fingers. The grass is green, flecked with tiny brown spots, and feels dry. I look right at Ralph, then I have to look away. 'It's a good idea, Ralphy. A great idea.' I even manage to grin at him, then I look back at my grass. 'I'll miss you. That's what's wiping me out, but I'll be okay, in a minute.' Tears prickle, my throat's packed tight.

'I'll miss you too, Lal, but – ' Ralph's voice is as soft as I've ever heard it. 'But this ain't the end of the line, eh? We're still mates, aren't we? We can work somethin' out. See what happens.'

I don't know what to say. I don't know what I'm being asked even. I don't want anything to end, whatever we've had, or whatever it is that we've got. Or might have. I look at the hand that's holding my wrist. It's hard to imagine how it could ever be the hand of a boxer, a fighter who made his living out of hitting people.

'Let me just have a few minutes to get used to the idea,' I say. 'All right? I just need a bit of time to level out.' So far I've managed to keep the tears back wherever tears come from, but I don't know how long I can keep it up.

Ralph's hand leaves my wrist and I go back to running my fingers along the grass stalk. I don't know about Ralph, but I'm thinking about us, pictures from other times and places running through my head as if I'm drowning – and maybe I am. Bloody feels like it. My life unravels before my very eyes: Ralph fighting in the tent, Ralph and me in my caravan, Ralph and me on the dodgem cars, Ralph and me brawling with the spotlighters, Ralph and me talking beside fires, bars, milkbars, rivers, bridges, Ralph and me –

The stalk of grass in my fingers breaks. I drop the pieces. They don't mean anything. I'm not about to read anything into one lousy piece of broken grass. Ralph and I've got history. We go back. We're friends, real friends – and friends just don't drop out of each other's life because one has to take a different way home. No, the world hasn't stopped. Look, I can hear sparrows in the peppertrees, can't I? And the sun's still warm and there's grass growing in the paddocks and I've got money in my pocket.

'Hey, Sly!' It's Knobs's voice.

I glance up at Knobs who's standing, looking down past the house to where a police car has turned up the driveway.

'Get your camera, mate. Check this out.'

Without making the decision to stand up I find I have. And so has everybody else outside. We watch the police car steadily climbing the slope, I hear the screen door rattle, Johnny comes across the yard, walking slowly as if he's baffled by what he's seeing. He looks at Jeff, Simon, and Knobs then he looks at Ralph and I.

'What's goin' – ' He doesn't finish.

Ralph stands with his hands on his hips and watches the white Commodore. It's dazzling, sunlight bouncing off it like it was a mirror. It stops ten metres short of us. The engine is turned off, I hear the handbrake go on. Doors open, two brawny policeman get out, putting on blue and white caps with big sun-browned hands. And then I see Simon and his Sony camera and everything falls into place like a guillotine dropping at the pull of a rope.

Tears of absolute rage blast out of my eyes. Suddenly I'm running and shouting.

'Simon, you bastard! You sly – ' I bend down, pick up a rock and throw it as hard as I can, missing Simon, but hitting the parked DTV Commodore with a loud smack. 'You cheating mongrel!' The anger in me is so vast I don't know what to do with myself. I want to hit, kick, bite, throw myself on the ground, swing with a stick, smash with a hammer, run, scream, kill. I scrabble for stones, desperately skimming my hands through gravel and grass, finding only sticks and pebbles. Suddenly Ralph's arms are around me, his hold unbreakable, hands locked, arms tight.

'Lal!' His voice is loud, his face right in front of mine. 'Hey, Lal! Lal, Lal – ' Now he shouts. 'Lal! Listen to me!'

I stop struggling, but I can't stop crying.

Those TV bastards! Tears wash down my face. I clench my fists until the nails tear skin. I can't stand it, I can't stand it, I can't stand it.

'Bastards!' I say again and again. 'Bastards!'

Ralph speaks right into my face.

'Lal! Listen!' He gets hold of my wrists now, and shakes them until my elbows bang hard into my ribs. 'Listen you, okay? I called the cops, not Simon. They didn't know anythin' about this. I called 'em, Lal, I did. You got that? Me.'

Deep sobs make me gulp for air. I try to fight them, then I just give in to them, and let them come as often and hard as they will. Ralph's words take hold.

'You did?' My voice comes out as a hoarse whisper. 'You called them? Why? Why?' Around me the world is gradually righting itself, trees standing up, clothes line stretching out, people drawing slowly back into focus.

Ralph lets go of my wrists. I rub my eyes and wipe my face with the side of my hand. And hiccough.

'Why'd you call them, Ralph? I mean – I dunno.' I don't know what I mean. Suddenly I'm exhausted.

'Lal – ' Ralph compresses his mouth into a buckled line, virtually a grin, and holds up open hands. 'I'm gonna sort this Echuca crap out once and for all.' He nods. 'Otherwise I couldn't ever have gone home. I'm just gonna tell 'em what I told you, and see what the law's gotta say about that. I've got to do it, Lal. You know that.'

I take a big breath and now Dell and Kate are beside me, their hands on my shoulders. I watch the two policemen walk slowly across the yard, their shoes so shiny they look blue. The biggest policeman, with three stripes on his shirt sleeve and a craggy face, watches the crew, giving no indication at all of what he's feeling. He ignores them, turns to Ralph.

'You Ralph Kiddle, mate?' The policeman's voice is as neutral as an announcement at a railway station, but the way he says 'mate' hints at authority that can be backed up instantly and effortlessly.

197

'Yeah,' says Ralph, now standing by himself, with all of us ringed around watching. 'I am.'

'Okay, Ralph – ' the policeman turns towards Simon again, seeming to be about to say something, then doesn't.

It's quiet now, although I can hear the stupid, ignorant, chirpy sparrows in the peppertrees. The sergeant and the other policeman, who both look twice as big as Ralph, stand a metre from him. Two onto one! my mind's saying. Not fair! But that's as far it goes. I don't utter a sound.

'Okay, Ralph, we wish to speak to you about the death of Ken Allen Corbett on or around the 18th of October, 1989, his body found in the Murray River at Gunbower Weir. We appreciate you contacting us about this matter, but I must also advise you that anything you do say in regard to this matter may be taken down and used against you in a court of law. Do you understand, Ralph?'

Ralph nods, biting his lower lip. I watch the younger policeman. Without making it obvious he seems to be staring at all of us at once, as if we might have guns. Of course we don't – but they do, dark brown wooden butts sticking up curved and ready from leather holsters. The sergeant continues. I watch the twin reflections of the sun on the rounded toes of the policemen's shoes, and listen.

'Ralph, you are entitled to contact your family, and to arrange legal representation. If you need assistance in obtaining a lawyer, we can arrange it – '

Kate's arm leaves my shoulder.

'Excuse me, sergeant, I – ' She starts to walk towards the two policemen. 'I'm a law student at . . .' Her voice falters. She doesn't seem to know where to look. She lifts a hand then lets it fall. 'No, I'm sorry, it doesn't matter, I guess I'm not able to . . .'

The sergeant stares at her, not unkindly really. When he does talk his voice is more like that of an ambulance officer than a police officer.

'He'll get everything he's entitled to, ah, madam. Don't worry. The law's our business. We do everything by the book, and then some.' There's no meanness in his face. Even his arms seem relaxed.

Kate nods, standing there for once in her life with less-than-dancing class posture. She seems to have wilted. And still those bloody sparrows chirp. They chirp on and on and on, until the sudden blasting of truck air horns grab the morning and fill it with their deep roaring.

I jerk around like everybody else has jerked around and see two trucks, one with a long grey trailer behind, the other loaded sky-high with pale green bales of hay. They turn into Barramah's front gate and start the long slow climb towards us, rumbling, growling, grunting as they go through gears, injecting black balloons of exhaust smoke into the clear air. Carter's Feed Carriers is printed on the grey trailer in red block letters. Jeff steps out of the shadow of the trellis, indicating to Knobs and Simon.

The TV crew move slickly, taking up positions so they can shoot the trucks coming up the slope. Jeff turns back to us, a smile loosening his face.

'Hey, Lal!' He holds up his hands as if to show me that now he really does have nothing left to hide. 'Fifteen tonnes of A-grade barley and five hundred bales of lucerne hay. Compliments of the viewers of DTV 5 News.' He then slaps Simon hard on the back as the cameraman kneels. 'Simon's idea, Lal! Gotcha!' He laughs and turns, concentrating on what his crew are doing.

Clunk. The penny drops. How bad do I feel? Real bad, about quite a lot of things actually.

*

Kate and I go for a walk. We walk up the hill behind the house and sit on rocks coloured pale green and orange by lichen. Around us the land unfolds: ploughed paddocks the colour of chocolate, paddocks the colour of dry straw, paddocks the colour of old cardboard, and trees with sheep and cattle resting in their shadows. The lightest of winds touches the backs of my hands. I'm tired, really tired.

'Thanks for trying to look after us down there,' I say, aware of the two big feed trucks parked nose to tail below us. 'I mean, I know it didn't quite work out, but I appreciated it anyway.'

Kate nods, fingers fiddling with a faded crimson gumleaf. The silence between us isn't uncomfortable. I don't try to break it. Eventually she does.

'For a minute down there I forgot I wasn't a lawyer,' she says. 'Then I remembered. Then I felt like a half-baked cake. Useless.' We glance at each other, then laugh.

'I felt like a bee in a bottle,' I say. 'God I was mad. I wanted to whack someone, like really hard. I've never been so mad. Or wronger, pardon the English. I'm good at that. Being wrong, I mean, not English.'

Kate drops the leaf and rests her arms on her knees. Her skin is golden.

'I think I'll go back and finish my course. Bake the cake, you know what I mean? Then maybe I might be of use to someone.'

So. It seems someone else has decided something for tomorrow, today.

'Yeah, use the old scone,' I say, which is something my gran used to tell me. 'It makes sense, doesn't it? You know it does.' It does. I try not to sound as if I'm feeling sorry for myself, even though I am. 'I'll just be happy,' I add, 'if I can be a bee that gets out of the bloody bottle. Buzz buzz buzz.'

Kate taps my knee with a single finger.

'I said you'll be right, Lal, and you will. You've got heaps going for you. And besides, you can always come to Sydney and stay with us forever. Now let's go get something to eat.'


I'm lying face down, staring out of the room I'm sharing with Kate when Jeff fills the vacant doorway. He knocks, even though it's obvious I'm awake.

'Can I come in? Or are you busy?' He looks and sounds amused, as usual.

'Yeah, I'm real busy.' I sit up, lean against the wall and sit cross-legged. I nod at the other bed. 'Sit down. I've run out of rocks.'

Jeff calmly sits on Kate's bed, cool in his white shirt.

'Look, about what happened today, Lal, I'm sorry. Sometimes what's supposed to be a surprise backfires. But that's showbiz. Still, sorry, eh?'

I collapse sideways onto the bed and push my face into the pillow. It muffles my voice and sends warm breath back up into my face.

'You're sorry?' I mumble. 'God, how d'you think I feel?' I turn my head so I can at least talk properly. 'God, I'm the one who did all the yelling and screaming. I'm the one who called Simon a mongrel.'

Jeff stretches his legs out so his boots hang over the end of the bed.

'Ah, he probably deserved it anyway, but – ' He holds up a small white card framed between his thumb and forefinger. 'I've got other fish to fry.'

I sit. My face still feels warm and rumpled from the pillow.

'Yeah, what sort of fish?'

Jeff hands me the card. It's got his name on it, below the DTV logo.

'A job's come up with me and the boys. Thought I'd give you the tip.'

My fingers crush the small cardboard rectangle. The word 'job' always gets my attention, especially when I haven't got one.

'What sort of job?' I try to straighten the card, but it'll never be the same.

Jeff assumes an even more laid-back position, clasping his hands behind his head, staring up at the paint-peeling ceiling.

'PA,' he says, turning his head to give me a cheesy grin.

'Yeah? What's that stand for?' I ask. 'Photocopier Ace?'

He laughs, and talks to a poem on the wall framed in warped plastic. 'Desiderata' it's called.

'Nah, Production Assistant. Someone to do some organis-ing, bit of typing, bit of research, bit of coffee-making. Pay's not real flash.' He stretches his elbows back. 'Better than drov-ing, though, I'd bet.'

A job . . . a job as juicy as a steak surrounded by golden brown chips, fried onions, fresh lettuce, and home-grown chilled tomatoes. A job. Suddenly someone whisks the plate away and tosses the lot to the dogs.

Do I really want to work at getting stories from people whose kids have been hurt or drowned or lost? Do I really want to work with people who shoot pictures of blood on roads after car smashes? Do I? No, not really.

Shut up, Lal, take the job and get the money.

No, hold on. Don't I want a job that *I* actually feel is gen-uinely useful? Isn't that why I've kept on moving and thinking and trying? Isn't that why I've hung out hoping and looking for so long? And why I'm still hoping and looking now?

Beggars can't be choosers, kid. And this job is a bloody good job. Ten thousand people would give their left arm for it. Just do it for a while then. Use it as a stepping stone. Don't burn your bridges. This might be the only bloody bridge you've got.

'I'm not sure, Jeff,' I say honestly, then do some knitting with my fingers. Jeff doesn't even look at me. He's reading the poem on the wall.

I tell him that the job really is a good job and that – words bounce out of my mouth like marbles clattering down concrete steps.

'But I'll have to think about it. Can you give me a day? I mean, what you guys do is kind of – ' How do I say this?

Jeff says it for me. 'Tacky, Lal?' He unfolds himself, swings his legs around, gets up, doesn't look offended.

'No,' I say, feeling my face screwing up. I don't want to insult this guy or his crew. 'No, it's not tacky. It's just you fellas concentrate on people who are in strife and I'm more interested in – '

Jeff bumps the light fitting with his head, sends it swinging.

'The good side?' He stops the light, shadows settle. 'Look, I understand. I'm not about to try it myself, but I understand.' He snaps out a finger. 'Think about it though, Lal. And ring me tomorrow. See ya.' He spins on the ball of one foot, stops, hand on the dinted doorknob, then smiles the TV-guy smile.

'You come onboard,' he says, 'we'd love to have you. You don't, then good luck, kid. You're a good dude, Lal. Call me, okay?'

'Promise,' I say. 'Tomorrow.'

The minute the door shuts all the fors and all the againsts line up on opposite sides of the room, then charge at me flat out. I duck for cover, my only protection a wrinkled white business card that offers me something, but I'm not quite sure what.

I'm in the bathroom, wet from the shower, looking at my bedraggled self in the mirror. My eyes are red, my hair looks flat and dull, I've got a spot on my chin, and my nose is peeling. Wonderful. There's a knock on the door.

'Be out in a sec,' I say, and wrap myself firmly in my towel. 'Just let me do my teeth.'

The green door opens twenty centimetres and two black hands appear, wrists up, fingers curled. A voice layered with mischief squeezes in alongside the arms.

'Look, Lal, no handcuffs. I'm a free man.'

I've taken myself and my diary for a walk through the paddocks. I sit on a rock that's like an island. How fitting! So here I am on my island, looking up at the old tin woolshed where Johnny will teach Ralph how to shear.

*7th May*

*Barramah Downs.*
*Weather: sunny, cool.*

*I'm proud of Ralphy, because pretty soon he'll be a beautiful shearer. He'll shear like he can box, with grace, guts, and speed. He'll pride himself on being as good as he can be, and he will be good. The Kiddle-kid's on his way and now the way is clear – because the Coroner's report found that he and the Riverman had nothing to do with the death of the guy in the weir.*

*The Coroner's report stated that Kenny Corbett died of Misadventure. In other words, it's thought he fell down the bank whilst drunk and got*

204

tangled in his own equipment. The only funny thing about the whole episode was that Simon had known of the finding for two weeks, and just assumed that somehow Ralph and I would know it too. Wrong. But not a problem any more.

From here I can see old Bett, the dogs, the horses, and hundreds of sheep as they wander from barley trail to muddy dam. A drought's a hard thing to finally break, though. Luckily, so are Johnny and Dell Hart. And today, so am I.

Today I feel strong, independent, and rich. In my pockets I've got Kate's address in Sydney, Ralph's family address in Echuca, a cheque from Johnny and Dell, four or five Minties, and Jeff's business card. Today I feel it's me who's in charge of my life. I'm in one of those rare places in time and space where I am perfectly happy exactly where I am. And from this place it feels like I can go anywhere and do anything – and maybe I can and maybe I will. But for now I'll just sit and enjoy.

Sure, later on I'll see what the afternoon brings, but until then it's indeed yours truly for the moment,

Lal J Godwin

# MORE YOUNG ADULT FICTION FROM PENGUIN

☆☆☆☆☆☆☆☆☆☆☆☆☆☆☆☆☆☆☆☆☆☆☆☆☆☆

### Looking for Alibrandi   Melina Marchetta

Josephine Alibrandi feels she has a lot to bear – the poor scholarship kid in a wealthy Catholic school, torn between two cultures, and born out of wedlock. This is her final year of school, the year of emancipation. A superb book.

*Winner of the 1993 CBC Book of the Year Award for Older Readers.*
*Winner of the 1993 Kids' Own Australian Literary Award (KOALA).*
*Winner of the 1993 Variety Club Young People's Talking Book of the Year Award.*
*Winner of the 1993 Australian Multicultural Children's Literature Award.*

### Came Back to Show You I Could Fly   Robin Klein

The moving and powerful story of eleven-year-old Seymour's friendship with the beautiful eighteen-year-old Angie. Beneath Angie's glitter lies the tragedy which is the world of drugs.

*Winner of the 1990 CBC Book of the Year Award for Older Readers.*
*Winner of the 1989 Australian Human Rights Award. Shortlisted for the 1990 NSW and Victorian Premiers' Literary Awards.*
*Now a feature film* (Say a Little Prayer).
*Winner of the 1992 Canberra's Own Outstanding List Award (COOL) Secondary Division.*

### The China Coin   Allan Baillie

Leah steps into China with her mother, loaded with her father's obsession about an ancient coin. But as they journey across this vast and bewildering land, they are drawn slowly towards the terror of Tiananmen Square . . .

*Shortlisted for the 1992 Guardian Children's Fiction Award, the 1992 NSW Premier's Literary Award and the 1992 SA Festival Award for Literature (Children's Books). Winner of the 1992 Australian Multicultural Children's Literature Award. A Children's Book Council of Australia Notable Book, 1992.*

# MORE YOUNG ADULT FICTION FROM PENGUIN

☆☆☆☆☆☆☆☆☆☆☆☆☆☆☆☆☆☆☆☆☆☆☆☆☆☆☆☆☆☆

**Queen Kat, Carmel and St Jude Get a Life**   Maureen McCarthy

A wonderfully passionate and absorbing novel about three very different girls in their first year out of school.


**Cross My Heart**   Maureen McCarthy

A vibrant, passionate, sprawling novel, set in outback Australia. The story of Mick and Michelle, chasing a dream, crossing their hearts for the future.

*Shortlisted for the 1993 NSW Premier's Literary Award (children's books). A Children's Book Council of Australia Notable Book, 1994.*


**Witch Bank**   Catherine Jinks

*'Nobody notices Heather. She may as well be invisible . . . '*

A humorous and quirky mystery with a dash of romance. Set in a large bank, the story is full of shrewd and funny observations about office life and magic.


**Lockie Leonard, Human Torpedo**   Tim Winton

Lockie Leonard, hot surf-rat, is in love . . . it has to be with Vicki Streeton, and it can only mean trouble, mega-embarrassment and wild, wild times.

*Winner of the WA Premier's Award, 1991.*

# MORE YOUNG ADULT FICTION FROM PENGUIN

☆ ☆ ☆ ☆ ☆ ☆ ☆ ☆ ☆ ☆ ☆ ☆ ☆ ☆ ☆ ☆ ☆ ☆ ☆ ☆ ☆ ☆ ☆ ☆ ☆ ☆ ☆ ☆ ☆

**Wilful Blue**   Sonya Hartnett

In this haunting novel, Sonya Hartnett brilliantly explores the inter-twined nature of talent and pain, and the mysterious and enduring bonds of friendship, love and memory.

**Sleeping Dogs**   Sonya Hartnett

The Willows are a dysfunctional family, and when one of the five children befriends an outsider who wants to uncover their secrets, the family's world is blown apart . . . Another powerful and disturbing book from this talented young writer.

**The Lake at the End of the World**   Caroline Macdonald

It is 2025 and the world has been cleared of all life by a chemical disaster. But then Diana meets Hector . . .

*Winner of the 1989 Alan Marshall Award, named an Honour Book in the 1989 CBC Book of the Year Awards and shortlisted for the NSW Premier's Award. Runner-up for the 1990 Guardian Children's Fiction Award.*

**Spider Mansion**   Caroline Macdonald

When the Todd family arrive at the Days' historic homestead for a gourmet holiday, they appear to be the most delightful of weekend guests. But weekend guests should know when to leave, and the Days realise too late that silently they have become enmeshed in a spiralling web of fear.

# MORE YOUNG ADULT FICTION FROM PENGUIN

☆ ☆ ☆ ☆ ☆ ☆ ☆ ☆ ☆ ☆ ☆ ☆ ☆ ☆ ☆ ☆ ☆ ☆ ☆ ☆ ☆ ☆ ☆ ☆ ☆ ☆ ☆ ☆ ☆ ☆

### The House that was Eureka   Nadia Wheatley

When Evie, Noel and Noel's grandmother come together in adjoining terrace houses in Sydney's inner city, something more powerful than a dream sets the past back in motion.

*Winner of the 1986 NSW Premier's Award for Literature. Commended in the 1986 CBC Book of the Year Awards. Shortlisted for the SA Premier's Award.*

### The Blooding   Nadia Wheatley

Seventeen-year-old Col is painfully initiated into the adult world, a world where right and wrong are inextricably linked and painful compromises must be made.

*An Australian Conservation Foundation Book Selection.*

### Landmarks   Nadia Wheatley (Ed)

Nine new stories by top Australian authors. Set against a variety of rural and urban landscapes, these stories explore the turning points in the lives of very different young people.

### The White Guinea-Pig   Ursula Dubosarsky

When Geraldine is entrusted with the care of her friend's white guinea-pig, Alberta, and when that guinea-pig mysteriously disappears, it is the beginning of Geraldine's growing up, and everything in her life changes.

*Winner of the 1994 New South Wales State Literary Children's Book Award and the 1994 Victorian Premier's Literary Award, and shortlisted for the 1994 CBC Children's Book of the Year Award – Older Readers.*